A Villa in Umbria

MARIANNE STEVENS

A catalogue record for this
book is available from the
National Library of Australia

ISBN: 1876922826
ISBN-13: 978-1-876922-82-5

Linellen Press
265 Boomerang Road
Oldbury Western Australia
www.linellenpress.com.au

Dedication

I was inspired to write this book when I travelled to Italy with my husband and we fell in love with an old house in Umbria. Up until that point, we had planned to buy somewhere in South West France, but when we saw how beautiful Umbria was, we changed our minds completely.

Having bought the house there, I spent many wonderful hours just breathing in the scenery and magic and felt compelled to write something to seal our love of the country and the people.

I would like to dedicate this book to the people who enhanced our lives in Umbria. Particularly to our Geometra, Marco and fantastic housekeeper, Lavinia, and to all the great friends we made there including the Mediterranean Garden Society. Lunch parties when we lingered under the shady pergola and seemed to go on forever. I now live near Perth, Western Australia but when I shut my eyes I am back there.

CONTENTS

Acknowledgments

To all the wonderful friends we made in Italy and those who helped us restore our beautiful stone villa. The garden I made is my legacy.

Prelude

Maggie's heart missed a beat as she scanned the latest bill for the renovation of the villa. Her lips thinned as she carried it out onto the terrace, her gaze stretching out across the Umbrian countryside, across the golden fields where the drone of machinery broke the silence, to the distant monastery where monks walked and prayed in silence. *Beautiful, beautiful Umbria.* She blew out a breath, fixed her gaze on the monastery hoping to draw inspiration from the monks within, hoping to gain strength from them. Taking a deep breath, she eased it out again then vowed she would fight on. She simply couldn't not lose all this.

A little gecko ran along the garden wall, paused near her hand then scurried on, its path pulling her attention from the land back to the terrace, and the villa, back to the work being done and the work still to do.

She had that morning been designing a website for holiday rentals and was anxiously waiting for the villa to be finished for she needed to take photos for the website. No one in their right mind would want to rent a house with half the roof unfinished and without a swimming pool. She sighed again. The villa didn't have to be perfect, just good enough for the photos to look impressive.

She scanned the house again, the invoice dragging at her thoughts. Everything seemed to cost more than the initial estimates: when the pool was being dug, they'd hit a snag. Because the pool was on a hill, and in an earthquake zone, the area had to be strongly reinforced, otherwise it could end up sliding down into the valley.

Then some enormous rocks had to be moved, and also a centuries old olive tree. Time meant money and the bills were adding up. It was strange really – while her aunt was well off, she obviously hadn't done her sums in connection with the restoration. Or perhaps she hadn't been as wealthy as everyone had thought.

Maggie's personal life was also in limbo: her relationship with the man she'd fallen in love with was quite fragile and now seemed to be going nowhere. After breaking up with Jonathan in Sydney she hadn't expected to be romantically involved with anyone for a long time, especially in Italy. Her ego had been so badly bruised back in Australia she wasn't on the lookout for another relationship. However, at 34 years old she didn't want to wait forever. So far she hadn't cared less about having children but she knew that it would eventually start to nag at her. Didn't someone say that 'life is what happens when you are busy making plans', or words to that effect?

She remembered her aunt saying: "Italians make wonderful lovers, but lousy husbands," but now she couldn't bear the thought of life without him, and Italy had woven its way into her heart.

When her beloved aunt died suddenly in Italy, leaving the villa to her, Maggie envisaged overseeing the restoration and putting it on the market as soon as possible. She imagined it would be a small interlude in her orderly life back in Sydney, and maybe a chance to see more of Europe. That was before she saw the beautiful old house, which she had fallen in love with at first sight. The renovations were, however, proving costly, and eating up the small inheritance she had been left. It was strange how life panned out. Why on earth hadn't her aunt bought a modernised property? Life would have been much simpler. *Mind you, the poor woman hadn't expected to die so suddenly either,* Maggie mused.

The man she had fallen for was a *Geometra* similar to an architect, a profession held in high regard in Italy. Maggie had met him in the

Notaio's office when she was signing the papers for the villa. It certainly wasn't love at first sight …

No, she shook her head, it had been the complete opposite. He appeared quite arrogant and dismissive of a young woman from Australia. He was tall, dark and, although not handsome, he had a special bearing about him that caught her eye.

Maggie had obviously not impressed him at the time, and being unable to speak Italian hadn't helped either. She had reciprocated those feelings too. *Who the hell does he think he is?* she had thought at the first meeting. *An arrogant man indeed!*

Maggie had considered dismissing him and choosing someone else to complete the work, as he had really rattled her cage. Her aunt, however, had thought him amazing and trusted him implicitly. Letters written to Maggie telling her about the villa were full of praise for the man. Her aunt had glossed over the fact that the roof needed replacing and the stonework needed repointing. She had written instead about the beautiful scenery, the peace and the friendliness of the locals. She had enthused about the fantastic views from the villa but hadn't mentioned the garden was a wilderness and putting in a pool was a necessity for holiday rentals. Her love of Italy had shone through in her enthusiasm and dream of restoring a villa in Umbria. Sadly she hadn't completed the renovations before suffering a sudden heart attack from which she never recovered.

It was now left to Maggie to fulfil that dream, and she so hated to lose a challenge.

Chapter One

'How about going out for a meal in the pub as this is my last night?' Maggie asked her flat-mates.

Their local pub, *Fiveways,* in Paddington, hummed with people as usual. As she looked around, Maggie wondered if she was doing the right thing, going to Italy. Paddington was one of her favourite areas in Sydney, with its beautiful old terrace houses and lacy balconies. Jetting off to the unknown had suddenly become a bit daunting. How could she leave the beautiful beaches and climate here? Although she was only working as a locum medical secretary, she enjoyed the variety of jobs she'd undertaken. The last one, with a medico-legal firm, though had not been the best job as she felt sorry for the patients going through the traumas with the rather hard-nosed lawyers and medical specialists. Most of the jobs were interesting and with pleasant people to work for, especially in the private gynae/obstetrics hospital.

'Well I think it's exciting, going to Italy," Ruth said wistfully. 'You will probably fall in love with some gorgeous Italian bloke.'

'Hmm. I think you should be careful of Italians. You might end up with a Mafioso like *The Godfather*!' Jan laughed at Maggie's shocked expression. 'Only teasing really, we are both as jealous as hell. Just think how romantic it would be.'

'Well, I suppose if I meet someone like George Clooney I wouldn't mind! Of course he's not Italian but he loves Italy and lives in Lake Como.'

The girls laughed. Maggie, however, had butterflies colliding in her stomach and needed a few more glasses of wine to stop stressing. It certainly was a big undertaking going to Italy and making her late aunt's dream come true. But, she shrugged inwardly, she could always return to her profession if it didn't work out. Medical secretaries, like legal secretaries, could work anywhere.

Checking through her carry-on bag the following morning, Maggie ticked things off. Thankfully, her late father who'd been born in the UK had insisted years ago that she had a European passport, and she thanked him for that now. She also had two hundred euros in cash, and enough dollars to pay for the taxi and any last minute things at the airport. In the bag were an adaptor plug and the chargers for her iPad and iPhone. The girls were going to sub-let her room until she returned, and she had told the agency she would be away for a while. So all was set.

At the airport book shop, Maggie flicked through a selection of guidebooks and bought a Lonely Planet guide to Umbria and also a small English/Italian dictionary, as well as a few paperbacks to read during her hotel stay.

That should get me started. Hopefully, she sighed, *I can get everything sorted out without too much hassle. Then I'll probably put it on the market … maybe go and work in London for a while before returning home.*

Her thoughts had been quite jumbled of late, everything happening so fast, so having some sort of plan settled them down.

Maggie boarded the Qantas flight to London and settled into her seat. The last few days had been extremely tiring and she sighed that she finally had time to relax. She clicked the seatbelt on and watched the bright lights of Sydney disappear below her as the plane roared into the night sky. The enormity of sorting out a building project in a foreign country while unable to speak the language prodded her gently, but she sighed again and thought, *if my old aunt was able to cope with it, surely I can cope with it. At least I have youth on my side.*

She sighed again, and in no time at all, fell asleep, exhausted.

Heathrow was its usual chaotic place, but holding a European passport helped speed her through. She pushed her way through the mass of people, collected her luggage and found her way outside the terminal to a bus that took her to Stansted airport, some way out of London. Here she boarded a Ryanair flight to Umbria, and slept the whole two hour flying time.

The small, hot Perugia airport moved at a much slower pace, passengers milling around happily greeting friends while collecting bags and suitcases which tottered precariously on a tiny luggage carousel. Maggie collected her luggage, and was welcomed to Italy by polite Italian officials. People gathered, eagerly waiting for passengers to arrive in a terminal where the air-conditioning was non-existent or totally inadequate.

Mopping her brow, she joined a queue at the rental car office, watched Panama-hatted Englishmen arriving – even men with shorts and sandals, some wearing socks! Maggie shuddered. *The English abroad!*

Glad to be out of the terminal building, Maggie loaded her suitcase into the boot of her little Fiat rental car, then returned to the building and bought a take away coffee and a bottle of water for the drive. How she needed that coffee! *Delicious!*

Now came the hard part: driving on the wrong side of the road. Nervously she pulled onto the road, watching the GPS closely as she negotiated a roundabout at the entrance to the airport. She flinched as cars tooted her impromptu changing of lanes. Then she was on the road heading away from the airport where rows of cypresses trees with their pencil lines reached up into the blue sky. She now had the chance to breathe again, her gaze drawn to the age of the buildings in the village as she passed through.

At a turnoff she joined a busy main road called the *Raccordo* which went in the direction of Firenze. Feeling like a tortoise on the inside lane of a fast moving racetrack, she gripped the steering wheel and drove steadily on, all the while being overtaken by fast moving cars and trucks. Constantly she checked that she was driving on the current side of the road

Nearing Lake Trasimeno, she decided to take a break and turned off and drove down a winding road to the lakeshore where few small boats and a ferry plied between the mainland and an island offshore. Pink and white oleanders framed the lakeside and everywhere happy people where packed into cafes that sold coffee and cold gelatos. Finding a parking space, Maggie slid the little car into it, paying the fee with euros she'd exchanged dollars for at the airport.

Savouring a gelato beneath a shady lime tree that overlooked the lake, Maggie watched children playing on the jetty. She scanned the two and three storey, brightly coloured buildings bordering the winding road along the lakeside, and a ruined castle that sat on top of the hill above the town. Across the road sat shops, cafes, and restaurants with shady canopies and quaint outside tables, and a smart looking boutique that advertised '*Deruta Pottery*'. It all reminded her of a seaside resort in the south of France, and she vowed to return here another day to explore further.

A loud church bell tolled the Angelus, and Maggie checked her watch. Everything closed down at lunchtime for the siesta period, she'd been told, so it was time to move on.

Climbing back into the car she thanked heaven for air

conditioning, like she did in Sydney summers, the thought making her wonder how everyone back home was getting on without her. While she didn't miss her last job, she did miss the camaraderie of her flat-mates. A lump formed in her throat as she gazed around the town one final time, suddenly feeling very much alone. Italy was the country of lovers, she sighed: how wonderful it would be to share this place with someone special.

Putting the car into gear, she continued towards her destination.

A few kilometres later, she reached Tuoro, a town the guidebook has said had a Hannibal connection. How fascinating to see the place she'd read so much about. She remembered visiting the oldest building in Sydney which was built in the 17th century, and here they talked about the Romans as if had been yesterday.

The town was siesta time quiet. Nothing stirred. She passed a boarded up news stall, a florists shop with the blind drawn down and a couple of hikers sitting outside a cafe. A few stray dogs wandered around but otherwise it was as if no-one lived there. Houses had their shutters closed against the sun as she drove slowly up the hill and along a road with pollarded trees. She almost missed the turning, the GPS's deep voice telling her at the last minute to turn off. This road meandered down through fairly modern houses until she came to a gateway. *The hotel, at last!*

Maggie parked under some shady trees and, leaving her suitcase in the boot, walked into the hotel's cool interior. A young girl stood behind the reception desk.

'Buongiorno,' Maggie said.

"Buongiorno, Signora and welcome to the hotel," the girl replied. 'My name is Martina. I hope you had a good journey here. Have you come a long way?'

Her mouth dropped open when Maggie told her exactly how far

she'd flown, and how many hours it had taken.

'You will want a sleep now, I think. May I have your passport please? I can then show you to your room where you can rest as long as you like. I will have Guido bring up your suitcase so don't bother carrying anything up.' She smiled, and Maggie was relieved the girl spoke English. 'Also if you prefer to have something to eat in your room later on, please let me know. There is already cool water in the fridge in your room.'

Her room had all she needed: a double bed – with a wrought iron bedhead and pretty white mosquito nets draped down either side – a small desk, an armchair and a large wardrobe, all contained within the chalky pink lime-wash walls with its decorative frieze around the top. The ensuite of walk-in shower and bidet was through an archway. Maggie remembered when she was a child holidaying in Italy she had thought bidets were children's basins or something for washing your feet. She smiled and sighed deeply – there was also a ceiling fan.

Martina explained how everything worked and Guido arrived with her suitcase, which he stowed on the luggage rack. The shutters had kept the room cool and Martina opened them partially to let the sunlight filter in.

The journey had exhausted her and she realised as Martina and Guido left the room how heavy her eyelids felt. She undressed quickly and sank onto the bed.

When she woke four hours later and looked out the window onto the sparkling waters of Lake Trasimeno in the distance, she immediately hunted through her luggage, found a pair of thongs, a cool cotton dress and her guidebook. The sun still shone, so it was time to explore, and more importantly she needed fresh air.

Closing the door behind her, she headed down the massive stone staircase to the ground floor, passed the reception desk and wandered into the garden. A gateway led to a crystal blue pool, beside which an elderly couple lounged in the sun, turning a dark shade of mahogany. Another younger woman reading a book looked up and smiled at her. The book was in German.

Wondering if any other guests were English-speaking, Maggie continued walking around the grounds. She came across the terrace, which was all set up with outdoor tables ready for the evening's dinner. Other tables sat within a large, beautiful conservatory. An elderly man, sitting in the shade nearby, doffed his Panama hat at her. 'Buonasera,' he said then again looking at her, hesitatingly said, 'Good afternoon.'

'Hello. Have you just arrived, and where have you travelled from?' he asked.

'Yes I arrived earlier this afternoon,' Maggie replied, realising he was English.

'Ah, that sounds like an Antipodean accent. Are you from Australia?'

'Yes. I've just flown from Sydney to London, and from there to Perugia. I couldn't get on a flight to Rome when I wanted to travel.'

'That sounds like an incredibly long journey! You must be exhausted.'

'Well,' she smiled, 'I managed a sleep just now for a few hours but I did manage to freshen up when I changed planes in Bangkok.'

'Do you know much about this part of Italy? I am glad to see you have a guidebook, which should give you the general gist of what has happened in this area since before the Romans. If you want to know anything more, I am writing a history of the area and the Battle of Lake Trasimeno. I am Geoffrey, by the way.'

'Maggie,' she reciprocated, smiling. 'There is so much to read about – I have only just touched the surface of it in my book.'

'Well you have probably heard of the battle here just outside the town when in 217 BC Hannibal defeated the Romans. He was a very clever young man. He lit beacons on the hill up there,'; Geoffrey pointed northwards. 'That is a town called *Castel Rigone* ... and so the Romans thought that was where they were holed up, when in fact they were down here surrounding a big field with the lake on the other boundary. When the battle was all over, the dead Roman officers were buried standing up in graves near here. Fascinating, my dear, just fascinating. Anyway, the crux of the matter was that they surrounded the Romans and their only escape was the lake where they were hacked to death or drowned.

'I am probably boring you to tears with all this!'

Maggie smiled and shook her head. She actually found it very interesting but there had been so much horror here in the past and in particular around the lake. How Italians lived amongst all this history she couldn't imagine as the past was so closely aligned with the present.

'Well, what are you doing here? Just holidaying?' Geoffrey asked.

'No, not really. My aunt died suddenly, leaving me a villa, not far from here. It was her dream to renovate it, and I would like to finish off what she started. I thought I would base myself here in the beginning, so I can deal with any problems on a daily basis. The villa isn't quite habitable from what I've heard; it is being re-roofed at the moment.'

'Good heavens. It sounds quite a task and coming from so far away must make it even more difficult. I'm afraid you will find there is a lot of bureaucracy here in Italy. They love stamping forms in the *postale* – the post office – and there will be mountains of paperwork to get through. I suppose you will have to get a permit to stay in Italy, being Australian? They used to make everyone do those but the European Union declared the rules illegal. Beforehand we had to queue for hours in the local police station to do so.

'Never mind, a good lawyer will get you through it. I also hope I didn't bore you talking about Hannibal but he is a pet subject of mine. Do you speak Italian?'

Maggie shook her head, and ruefully wondering if the Latin lessons she'd had at school would help. She could just remember '*Amo, Amas, Amat*' and that was about it. Perhaps it would come flooding back if she learnt some Italian. 'But I am lucky. I have a European passport so I can stay here without a visa.'

'Well that is a very useful thing! I have been staying here for a few weeks, and will no doubt be here until the end of the month. You might have heard of the earthquake a few years ago which devastated Assisi and killed people. Sadly some of the priests went back into the basilica after it happened. Then the aftershocks brought more stuff down around them and they were in the wrong place at the wrong time.

'I didn't know about that. Heavens, what a terrible thing,' Maggie replied.

'The basilica there is absolutely beautiful and has been painstakingly restored. You must visit it one day. My own home was damaged but it has taken many years to sort out the insurance claim as dealing with Italian bureaucracy is always a long and tedious process.'

After an interesting time spent discussing history with Geoffrey, Maggie returned upstairs, unpacked till she found her swimsuit – the rest could wait until the next day. What she needed now was a swim to reinvigorate her.

It wasn't as hot as earlier but there was a beautiful early evening light similar to Australia. Kicking off her shoes, she flipped out a towel on the sun lounge, dropped her sunhat and book on the chair, and dove in, the water folding round her like silk. She swam a few leisurely lengths, still finding it hard to believe she was here in Italy and not back in the cooler climes of Sydney.

Finger combing her wet hair back, Maggie returned to her sun lounge. She wanted to enjoy this period of relaxation before tackling the real business of sorting out the villa. Picking up her book, she read the first few pages but then found herself almost slipping into sleep. The sound of a dog barking woke her and she looked at her watch. The sunburnt couple still lay on their sun loungers, and the German woman was lazily doing laps in the pool. A young woman with a small dog had just entered through the gate and was heading towards an empty sun lounger. The sun would be going down soon and she struggled to stay awake so decided to go up to her room and have a light snack sent up to her.

The next day she spent lazily, lying around the pool, swimming and reading her guidebook, jet lag taking its toll. Her brain felt woolly and she was glad she wasn't meeting the lawyer until the following day; glad she could enjoy the peace and quiet … until a young family came back from their day touring around Florence. Two squabbling children splashed noisily in the pool, probably thankful to be doing that rather than dragging themselves around hot city streets.

Maggie lay on her chair, thinking about her meeting with the lawyer and perhaps seeing the villa. She wondered about the geometra, who she visualised as elderly, a charming, older man perhaps reading between the lines from her aunt's letters. What had seemed to be an adventure now appeared a monumental task to her. She hoped he spoke English and remembered her aunt praising him and saying she couldn't have done anything without his help.

That evening, Maggie sat at a table close to the open doors of the conservatory, listening to the harpist playing outside. The terrace, bathed in a soft golden, evening light, lent an air of magic to the surrounds. She loved the way newcomers politely murmured 'Buonasera' to everyone as they entered the restaurant. After a delicious meal, she yawned, obviously still adjusting to the time difference. Then she climbed the stone stairs to her room, quickly brushed her teeth and fell into bed. She was asleep almost immediately.

Chapter Two

Next morning when Maggie came down to breakfast she accepted Geoffrey's offer to join him at his table, and labored over her choices – fresh fruit and yoghurt, including a coffee-flavoured one; cakes and croissants, called *cornetto*. Opting for fruit and yoghurt she asked the waitress for coffee, as she sat down.

'If you want a flat white, as you call it in Australia, just ask for a *cappuccino sensa schuma*. It means coffee without the foam,' Geoffrey said.

'Oh great, thanks. I love my coffee and the Italians make wonderful coffee, don't they?'

'Yes, the worst coffee is in England so if you go there, you will find they seem to boil it! I am so glad you are doing all this legal work properly too,' he said. 'Your aunt will have met with the lawyer in the beginning when she bought the house. The Notaio would have given her a translated copy of the contract, but also read the document out aloud in Italian to her. That is the law here. It is also quite charming.

'In Italy so many ex-pats try and cut corners. They build things or put in a pool without permission and years later find they can't sell their properties. They have to go through all the boring stuff they should have done in the beginning. Your aunt was wise to have a good *geometra* … a surveyor, to guide you through the process.'

Maggie was pleased to hear that. Throughout the meal she kept a watch on the time and eventually excused herself, returning to her room to check her make-up and tidy her medium length bob. She was pleased that her suntan had come back and that her hair looked neat and shiny as she wanted to make a good impression on the lawyer and the geometra on their first meeting. She studied herself in the mirror. Though not overly tall, she was slim, her figure carrying the hairstyle well. She was glad she hadn't had it cut any shorter, for this style suited her, and Jeffrey, her previous boyfriend, had always loved her glossy auburn hair. She shrugged, not really wanting to think about him again. He had let her down badly and she was pleased to have left him behind.

After consulting her map, Maggie punched the address into the *Sat Nav* and set off for *Citta di Castello* where she would meet the lawyer, a *Notaio*, at 11 am. The GPS voice directed her till she parked beneath the big, shady trees outside the town's ancient walls. The meeting was inside the beautiful palazzo a short walk away, inside the imposing building built of honey-coloured stone and adorned with impressive statues. The Italian flag hung limply from a flagstaff.

On entering, the receptionist took her upstairs to the second floor, the *secondo piano* in Italian. Opening the door, the receptionist introduced her to the distinguished looking man sitting behind the desk, an elderly man in a smart suit and silk tie. The lawyer rose and greeted her in well pronounced English and gestured for her to be seated.

'Welcome, Signora. I am so sorry to hear about your aunt; she was a delightful woman. I met her a few times when we were dealing with the sale of the villa and now there is just some paperwork to be completed, to make sure everything is put into your name. It was very sad she died before she had done all the work she wanted to do. The geometra will be here shortly. Perhaps you would like a coffee while we are waiting for him?'

Maggie said she would love one and the receptionist hurried out to make it. Before she returned, a rap came on the door and a tall man in his late 30s strode in. He said good morning in Italian to the lawyer and nodded to her. Maggie rose from her chair and they shook hands.

'Antonio Gentile,' he said rather abruptly. This was the geometra, a much younger man than she'd expected. Dark haired with rather sultry eyes, his stern expression seemed most unfriendly. He also didn't seem impressed that Maggie didn't speak Italian. The lawyer explained to her that everything was almost finalised and she had one other paper to sign. This was translated into English on the desk in front of her.

Reading it, she took out her pen and signed it. He explained that Antonio Gentile would supervise the restoration work, unless she chose otherwise. Her aunt had sensibly organised the most important work, including the roof and electrics. He carried on talking about the small inheritance she would receive and trusted it would cover all the restoration work.

The receptionist returned with a tray carrying three cups of black coffee and a bowl of sugar. She asked if anyone would prefer milk but Maggie decided she would have hers black like the others. Finding it slightly bitter, she added sugar. Stirring her coffee, she glanced at the geometra, wondering why he was so standoffish. Maybe he didn't like dealing with women, or perhaps just Australian women. He stood looking down at her, which made her feel uncomfortable.

'Well, what happens next?' she asked the two men.

The lawyer smiled. 'I think it's up to Antonio here to advise you regarding the building works and he should carry on as he has been doing. Obviously there is no need for you to stay in Italy if you have pressing business to return to in Australia. If you open a bank account locally, the money can be paid into it for you. Anyway, you must excuse me, Signora, as I have to be in court shortly.'

With that, he shook her hand, and Antonio's, and left them facing each other in the room. Maggie swallowed thickly. She didn't even know where the villa was or what was involved. Uncertainties piled on top of her and she felt tired; forced back the tears in her eyes. The lawyer was a lovely fatherly figure but this geometra guy looked stiff and grumpy. He obviously wanted to be elsewhere and not stuck with some woman he didn't know.

Antonio briskly picked up his briefcase then turned to her. 'Perhaps we should have a light lunch in the city to discuss matters,' he suggested.

She nodded, feeling somewhat overwhelmed and sad that her aunt wasn't here to carry on what she'd started. The atmosphere felt tense and awkward and, although she wasn't too keen on having lunch with him, she thought it wise to talk about the work on the villa. She wondered what bothered him – what made him so unfriendly.

They moved downstairs and turned left outside the building; stepped into a narrow street with two or three cafes situated in the shade. Antonio chose one and guided her to a table beneath a large umbrella. He nodded to various acquaintances who looked approvingly at the young woman beside him. Maggie thought if only they knew he was here under sufferance.

'I would like to express my condolences on the death of your aunt. She was a very pleasant woman and very capable. She had good ideas regarding the restoration work and didn't want to destroy its historical feeling, unlike many foreigners.'

Surprised he had liked her aunt, Maggie murmured her thanks, yet clenched her teeth at the impression that 'capable' was not something he had seen in her. From the manner of his speech, she surmised English was his second language.

A waiter brought them cold water each, and menus in Italian.

Maggie looked at it then sighed.

'Would you prefer fish or meat? It is served with pasta or you might like a salad?'

Maggie demurred. She didn't mind what she ate today. She had little appetite. 'I'll let you choose.'

The meal was simple but beautifully cooked, tiny portions of fish in delicate breadcrumbs and a delicious salad of rocket and mozzarella cheese. Beside them on the cobbled street, a small amount of traffic entered the town through an ancient stone gateway, and every so often a little three-wheel truck or a scooter would pass. In the distance she heard a strange siren, very loud and distinctive, and nothing she had heard before.

'That is an ambulance. The hospital is just across the road.'

'What vehicles are allowed to drive in here? I thought I saw 'No entry signs' by the old walls when I drove up?' Maggie asked him.

'Local drivers who have special stickers on the windscreens can come in, and of course delivery vehicles, but it's the same in many small towns in Italy. It's to stop traffic coming in and spoiling them.' Then he changed the subject.

'So why have you have ended up here to take over what your aunt started? It's a long way from Australia?' he queried. 'Do you just want to see how things are progressing before returning back there?'

'I really didn't have much choice about coming over. My aunt died suddenly from a heart attack, as you know. I had a phone call from the lawyer, and then I found out about the villa. I have not even seen it yet and have no idea how much needs doing. Unfortunately my aunt had no other family, and seeing my parents have passed on I was the last one left. We were very close.'

'Well we can soon fix up showing you the villa. I will take you tomorrow and go through things with you. Let me know where you are staying and we can meet up half-way.'

Maggie's eyebrow rose subtly. Antonio seemed to be thawing out a bit.

'It's a pity you don't speak any Italian though,' he said rather off-handedly.

'I will definitely be taking lessons if I do decide to stay here. I just want to look at the villa and see how it is progressing.'

Lunch passed pleasantly enough, Antonio's initial frostiness seeming to thaw again as the meal progressed. Perhaps, Maggie thought, he thought she was just another foreigner ready to exploit the country. She actually sensed he thought her a spoilt young woman who had inherited the villa, which was far from the truth.

'I presume you will want us to finish the restoration and then put the villa up for sale?'

Her annoyance already provoked, she replied pointedly, 'I don't know until I see the house. I can't make up my mind until then and I am also not sure about the financial situation. I know from letters I received from my aunt that she intended to live in the smaller house and let the villa out in the summer.'

Antonio sighed. 'Well, we shall see. It's rather difficult coming from Australia for you to deal with this I think, and of course not speaking the language either.'

Inwardly seething, Maggie's jaw set. She said nothing. Antonio insisted on picking up the bill and they made plans to meet the next morning at the villa, Maggie assuring him she could find her way with the aid of the Sat Nav.

'Where did you learn to speak such good English?' she asked him before they left.

'My mother is English and my father is Italian. I learnt to speak both languages at home. Being in a profession in Italy, it is also essential to speak English.'

No wonder his English is so good, Maggie thought. *He speaks it without any trace of an accent.'*

When she returned to the hotel all was quiet. Only the bees lazily buzzed amongst the oleanders and the hotel cat lay dozing under a large fig tree. Walking to the front door, she glanced up at the building's magnificent façade, admired the stunning fanlight over the front door. It must have been home to a wealthy family in the past, she thought as she opened the door and stepped into its cool interior. Italians sensibly kept all the shutters and doors closed, keeping the sun and heat out. She picked up her room key from the desk and, seeing no one was around, crept quietly upstairs to her room. Her bed had been made and all was neat and tidy and she quickly changed into a swimsuit.

She thought back to her conversation with Antonio: *What an insufferable man!* She hadn't come across someone who put her back up quite as much nor as quickly as he did. She decided to prove him wrong, and decided she would have Italian lessons as soon as possible, and also look up short-term rentals on the Internet. Of course she was rushing the gun, as she had seen neither the villa nor what a ruinous state it might be in. Staying in the hotel would make her money disappear too quickly, she had realized, and a self-contained apartment might be better … if she stayed on. It would be sad to leave this beautiful place but she had to make her money last. Not knowing how long all this would take also was a big problem.

The evening meal was unusual: scrumptious zucchini flowers fried in olive oil followed by a plate of pasta parcels with a sprinkling of thyme. Taking a glass of wine, she sat outside on the terrace,

21

listening to a nightingale whilst an owl hooted hauntingly in the trees. The dark, velvet sky was peppered with stars and a full moon shone overhead, revealing Lake Trasimeno shimmering in the distance.

Chapter Three

The next morning after breakfast, Maggie drove off to see the villa, her impatience and apprehension growing about what she might discover. Driving through the beautiful Niccone Valley with its fields of tobacco plants and vibrant yellow sunflowers bordering the road with their heads turned towards the sun was pleasant. Old stone towers poked up on some houses – for drying tobacco leaves she had learned from her guidebook. She passed an *ape*, a three-wheeled vehicle, its occupants overflowing over the side of the strange contraption, which made her smile. The elderly couple, obviously on their way to market, happily sauntered along the country road, oblivious to anyone else. The old man drove, his rather stout wife, carrying an enormous straw basket on her lap, squeezed in beside him.

Following the winding road, Maggie drove beside the railway line until she reached the outskirts of a big town. Here the strident tones of the Sat Nav told her to turn right under a railway bridge. This road wound way up into the hills, passing a beautiful old stone castle and a few more open fields bordered by ancient olive trees. She found the village, which was just a cluster of houses, and a bar that sadly no longer opened – there was not even a disused church.

At the fork in the road, she made a quick right-hand turn and drove slowly up a white, dirt road, creating dust clouds as she went. Finally she reached the end and parked in the shade of a huge tree. A large Peugeot car was parked beside the wall and Maggie guessed it was Antonio's. A couple of small trucks and an *ape* were also parked in the shade, and the sound of hammering came from within the grounds.

Her car had set the local dogs to furious barking, something the guidebooks never mentioned, even though dogs seemed to be everywhere in the countryside. She heard a young girl's voice yelling '*Silenzio*' and the barking quietened down. Just then a cockerel crowed and a neighbouring one answered it from across the valley. *It's extremely rural here*, she realised, *so unlike Sydney. What a strange place for auntie to buy a house.*

Maggie took a deep breath and approached the doorway, wondering what awaited her through the opening.

Antonio had obviously heard the car door slam and the dogs barking. He came out a side gate, frowning, yet not looking quite so unwelcoming as the day before. He greeted her in a much more friendly fashion. Wiping his dusty hands on his trousers, he ushered her inside.

'I trust you slept well? That is a very well-known hotel where you are staying and the food is very good. Is it to your liking?'

'Yes, it's delightful and will be hard to leave there when I do. I love finding out about all the history of the area, and there's a historian staying there who has been explaining it all to me.'

'Yes, I have often dined in that hotel. I am glad you are enjoying the history of the area as well. Lake Trasimeno is very famous of course.'

He gestured that she follow him through a tall doorway. Maggie stopped, amazed at the stunning view in front of her. From the other end of the terrace where she had entered, the garden dropped down, and below were fields of patchwork colours, and hills disappearing into the distance.

The largest hill to her right appeared to have a cross on top, and a noisy, cranky old tractor worked in the fields below. Maggie knew right then why her aunt had fallen in love with the house, the view equally taking her breath away. Then she turned and viewed the house with its rather sad-looking exterior. Plaster rendering hung off the walls and it looked like damp had darkened the stonework. Bits of ivy clung to the windowsills and the roof looked definitely in poor shape. She glanced at the garden, a mass of waist-high weeds with trees dotted around them. *Obviously uncared for.*

'Has that high hill got a name? It looks fascinating. And what is the building on the other hillside?' she asked him.

'That is Monte Acuto and you can climb to the top sometime. The other building over there is a beautiful old monastery. Anyway, welcome to the villa. I am sorry, it must be sad for you to see it without your aunt. The amount of work we have to do is not that tremendous and it looks much worse than it is. Once the roof is made sound, everything will be more easily sorted. You can see we are taking off the rendering and restoring the beautiful stonework. The previous owners only came in the summer so weren't fussed about the condition of the roof. It was quite habitable for the summer months as it doesn't rain then. They also used a couple of goats in the garden to eat up the weeds. There are men working on the roof at the moment and they are over halfway through. We are insulating it and replacing the old roof tiles.'

At a loss for words, Maggie simply nodded. She followed him inside and, as the shutters were all closed, her eyes had to adjust to the dark. Antonio hurriedly opened them so she could see the room properly.

The floor was constructed of old brick tiles laid in a herringbone pattern and huge dark beams supported the ceilings, both making the house look solid. A couple of arches led to an old-fashioned kitchen that was and not much more than a passageway, but it did have a dishwasher and a rather nondescript cooker. She followed

Antonio through the second arch into a bathroom and a laundry area. Antonio gestured to her to follow him upstairs.

Four large bedrooms and a couple of bathrooms, complete with loos and bidets but only showers over the baths, spread out across the upper floor.

'How old is the house? Do you know anything of its history?'

'Well, it is at least three hundred years old, and was originally owned by the monks from the monastery on the hill.'

'How fascinating. Anything else?'

'Downstairs is where they kept the animals, which kept the house warm in winter. It was pretty much the same all through Italy.'

'I don't like having baths with showers over them. Would it be very expensive to change them to walk in showers? Perhaps only have one bath in the house in case children might want to use it?'

'Yes that wouldn't be too expensive as we have to re-tile the bathrooms anyway,' he replied.

'If it's anything like Australia it's not good to use too much water and I guess the climate is dry in the summer?' she queried.

'Yes, I agree. It is also safer for people when you let the house to have a proper shower. However, you are on mains water here which is good. Electricity is the most expensive thing you will find too.'

She followed Antonio downstairs, where this time he turned the other way into a large bedroom with en-suite bathroom. This was obviously where the old couple had slept when they owned it. It was in a better decorative state than the rest of the house and there was a walk-in shower.

'There is one other place of interest to you, so please follow me.' Antonio led the way out through the back of the kitchen, through a doorway into what had once been a vegetable garden. Before her stood a small cottage, which Antonio went on to explain might be a good place for her to live if she wanted to stay here. It was her aunt's plan to do so. She could let the main house out to tourists and keep an eye on things, yet be private.

'As I said, it was what your aunt envisaged she would do. She liked the idea of a small but tucked away property for her to live in, so that she was on the spot in case of problems. Of course you probably want to sell it. It's rather a big project for a young woman to deal with. I am sure you must want to go back to Australia,' Antonio said rather disparagingly. 'You could even sell both buildings separately if you wish.'

'Please don't be too hasty! I may well decide to run it myself as a business. I have yet to make those decisions yet,' she responded curtly.

Antonio shrugged his shoulders in a very Italian manner and his eyebrows lifted at her remarks.

'We shall see,' he said just as curtly. 'I will show you inside the cottage. You can then make up your own mind, but you would probably be better to sleep on it.'

The high-ceilinged, L-shaped building was all on one level and plain. A large living room opened onto the kitchen area and a bedroom with its own bathroom. Two smaller bedrooms and another bathroom seemed very light and airy. The cottage could also be reached by a small lane from a slightly different direction, which meant her car wouldn't be a nuisance to people staying in the house. In the weed-infested courtyard was the remains of a good-sized goldfish pond which she envisaged could easily be converted to a swimming pool.

Maggie brightened at this. She always loved the water, and being able to swim whenever she wanted was definitely a drawcard. Even if it were only a plunge pool, she would be happy.

She envisaged an Arab style house, rather like the Moorish ones she'd seen in Spain years ago, where the walls of the house and garden surrounded a cool, inviting pool.

They walked back through the house onto the terrace. Eyeing the garden, Maggie asked Antonio about putting in a pool for guests there. She gathered it would be a necessity if she wanted to rent it in the summer.

'A pool is definitely a good idea. We would have to get permission of course from the Commune.'

'What is the commune?' Maggie asked.

'Ah, the local authority, what you probably call Council back in Australia.'

'What about designing the garden? It's in a real mess right now.'

'I can get some quotes for you as you would need pathways and maybe a pergola or something at the end of the pool.'

Maggie smiled. She could see herself here in a pool with a glass of Campari in her hand. She was sure she would be inundated with friends from Australia, all keen to enjoy a free holiday in Umbria. She imagined flowers and a pool with chairs alongside and perhaps some sun umbrellas. However, she knew she couldn't contemplate freeloaders – the house had to pay its way.

'Well, I am getting carried away. We really ought to discuss the house and what work is ongoing. I can see you have started on the roof, which I guess my Aunt approved.' Maggie had seen about three young workmen chiselling away at the stonework outside, as well as a couple renovating the roof.

'The main work has been approved and also the money put aside for the roof, so that will help. You will have to work out how much you want to spend on the pool and garden. I think you should come to my office in town and I can go through all the plans with you now you have seen the villa. If you are serious about a pool, we will have to put in an application quickly to get the work done before the start of the season too. I can also give you some idea of costs.'

'Would you like to do that now or another day?' Maggie asked, grabbing the bit between her teeth with keenness to start the project. What she'd imagined as a ruin wasn't as bad as she'd thought. To save money she could design the garden herself, but she needed to get an idea of all the other costs involved as she was starting to worry hard about that.

'I am available now if you would like to follow me down the hill to my studio in town. We can go through everything there in air-conditioned comfort.'

Maggie agreed and, with a last look at the wonderful view, walked out to her car. *What a huge project! Can I cope with it?* she wondered before smiling grimly. *I will if it kills me – just to show that arrogant damned Italian what Australian women are capable of!'*

Driving back down the hill, she followed Antonio's car and turned right at the bottom onto a road that led them into town. It was market day, and therefore very busy. Cars and bikes were everywhere, bikes tending to go up and down one-way streets whichever way they chose. Thankfully, Antonio's building had a big car park, well shaded in one corner. She squeezed her car in beside his and together they walked through the doorway to his design studio. A young woman smiled and asked if they would like coffee to which they both replied "Yes".

The building was obviously very old but creatively renovated with flair. The studio was beautifully cool, the floors covered in stunning Italian tiles. Maggie sat down by Antonio's drawing board where he opened up sheets of plans and spread them out on the table in front of her.

'Now these are what your aunt and I planned to do, but now you are in charge you may of course wish to change them. As you saw this morning, the old roof tiles are being removed, then the roof is insulated and the old ones put back, keeping with tradition.'

'Thank you. I will look and see what you have here first but I expect whatever my aunt chose will be good. She had amazing taste. However, I need to know how much has been paid for and what the future costs will be.'

Maggie was pleased to see she could read the plans quite easily and the only changes she wanted to make were in the kitchen.

'What about water and sewerage?'

'You have a septic tank in the garden but thankfully the house is on mains water.'

Maggie breathed with relief. That was something! 'What about irrigating the garden?'

'There is an old well somewhere around here," he pointed to a place on the plan, "so that could be used and a drip-feed system installed. Now the other thing is we have had to increase the electricity into the house to 6 kilowatts. Most Italians have only 3 kilowatts in their homes, and if someone uses a hairdryer and the washing machine is on, the fuses will blow.'

'Good heavens, how archaic!' Maggie retorted then realised that probably wasn't the most diplomatic thing to say to an Italian. 'Do I have to sign anything else for you to keep going, Antonio?' she asked, trying to change the subject.

'Well not yet, but when I get the forms for the application for the pool you will have to sign those and come with me to the commune to talk to the official there. Also if you want to change the old pond into a small pool.'

'I definitely want to change the kitchen. I would like a big kitchen with a large working area and a range-type cooker. I want to buy a gas barbecue, as most people would expect one. I think people renting the house would want a better kitchen than this one.'

'Well you can either have a kitchen built by a local carpenter or buy a readymade one from IKEA or somewhere. In an old house the walls are not only very thick but often not straight, so it might be easier and cheaper to have one custom-made,' he told her. 'Also if you wanted to sell the villa, a beautiful kitchen would make it more saleable.'

Maggie rolled her eyes, and gathered her things together. Now that the most important decisions had been made she decided it might be a good idea to look around the market in the local town; get her bearings before heading back to the hotel. She thanked Antonio and was glad she would soon start her Italian lessons. The thought that Antonio didn't think she could manage a project like this really infuriated her, and while she obviously needed his help, she wanted to finish the villa in memory of her beloved aunt.

Parking in town was a bit of a nightmare, cars often 'abandoned' rather than neatly parked. Maggie decided to use an ATM she noticed up a one way street and was nearly knocked flying when a woman riding a bike came hurtling towards her the 'wrong way', but then, to Italians, rules probably meant they were for someone else not them! Thankfully the ATM gave her the option of transacting in English, which made it easy. The market was a different story; very lively and full of fascinating stalls, queues built up at the *porchetta* stalls and the smell of freshly cooked pork tantalized the palate. In fact Maggie retraced her steps, and joined a queue to buy porchetta in a bread roll for lunch. She found the cheese stall, pondered over the different varieties she had never heard of, and guessed some were probably either sheep or goat's milk. Gorgonzola she recognised but *pecorino* was a new name to her. The stallholder, in broken English, told her it was sheep's cheese. There were meat and vegetable stalls around which Italian women bustled, pushing shopping trolleys. At one stall a fat man smoked a cigarette, which quite put her off. She noticed a smart, uniformed official going around checking receipts and it was obviously important to be given one, otherwise the stallholder could be in trouble. Surprised at such bureaucracy, Maggie had imagined Italians were a bit more lax about such matters. She thought guests staying at the villa would love to buy food here in the market. Flowering plants were for sale all over the place, potted red geraniums and multi coloured petunias seemed a favourite as well as large pots of brilliant pink oleanders and small olive trees. The biggest queues were for vegetables as the locals obviously liked to grow their own.

Drifting over to the square, Maggie noticed a bank called *the Banca Monte dei Paschi di Siena. What a wonderful name,* she thought. *Perhaps I should open an account there.*

As she returned to her car, she caught a glimpse of Antonio in the square walking beside a very elegant and attractive young woman. They entered a nearby café. '*Well he is human after all.*' However, why did she not feel happy about that? Maybe the fact that he didn't take any interest in her as a woman, suddenly crossed her mind.

Feeling a bit miffed, and also very hot, Maggie decided a swim and a siesta would cure her mood and, returning to her very warm car, opened up all the windows. Then she sat and ate the delicious porchetta bun. The air conditioning cooled her skin as she drove back through the stifling heat, back past the tobacco fields, thinking how incredible to be still growing that loathsome crop, and how many lives would be ruined smoking the darned stuff.

Back at the hotel, she changed into her swimsuit and, taking her book with her, walked over to the pool. Geoffrey sat in the shade of the only large tree nearby and smiled at her.

'Good morning, or is it afternoon?' he asked. 'How did you get on with the villa and all the work that might need to be done?'

'Well, I have had the most amazing time being shown it by the geometra. A lot of work is being done on it but it will be beautiful one day. The scenery there is wonderful too. So beautiful. I took some time exploring the town as well, and the market there. It was so full of life and wonderful fresh food. I loved it.'

'Well Italians love their food. Even the young school children are given a menu to take home for their parents to check out for the following week! Food and its quality are drilled into them at an early age here in Italy. If the parents don't approve, then they have to change the menu!'

Maggie remembered her school lunches in Australia – usually Vegemite or Peanut Butter sandwiches, and a piece of fruit. What a different lifestyle they had here in Italy.

'In my boarding school in England, we had hot dinners.' Geoffrey reminisced. 'We loved steak and kidney pudding or toad in the hole. The Italians wouldn't be impressed!'

Maggie laughed. 'Well if you will excuse me, I am going to have a swim and relax. Perhaps one day you would like to come and see the villa for yourself,' Maggie offered.

Delighted, Geoffrey gave her a wave and settled back with his book.

Maggie smiled. After worrying herself sick about what she would find, she felt happier now that it wasn't an old ruin, and she loved its location. Wandering over to a nearby lounger she dropped her book onto the table beside it. She couldn't wait to jump into the refreshing, salt-water pool – no chlorine. Doing laps, she thought about her morning and the work still to be done on the villa. It was actually quite exciting and she began to understand how her aunt had fallen in love with Umbria. The big question mark however was how much would all the work cost and, more crucially, would it be ready for the summer season? How she would hate to be defeated and allow that arrogant geometra to be right. He obviously had no faith in her ability to carry on. Her teeth clenched. *Loathsome man,* she thought.

That evening, like the last, Maggie enjoyed the superb food at the small hotel where she felt welcomed, and picked up a few more words of Italian. Her lessons with Gina, whom she had telephoned, would start next week in the local town. She vowed she would prove that infuriating man wrong, and not only learn Italian but sort out the villa if it was the last thing she did.

The next few mornings, she drove up to the village. The skilled Neapolitan builders sang lustily as they worked on the villa, and at lunchtime they built up a small fire and cooked their meals. The small kitchen was fine for odd snacks so Maggie made coffee for the workmen, which they drank very strong. Her mouth dropped open when they poured sachets of sugar into the little mocha pot before stirring the mix.

Walking outside, she ran her hands over the stonework – it was coming on beautifully. The roof had been repaired, and the old tiles re-installed after insulation had been fitted. To an outsider, it looked just as it had been before. The dreadful rendering was almost all chipped off, transforming the house. At one stage, Antonio and Maggie were asked to inspect the work but Maggie thought the stonework looked flat and didn't have the right effect. She asked Antonio to suggest they 'brush out the mortar.'

When it was done, it looked perfect, each stone standing out on its own. Before, it had almost looked like a new building and even Antonio looked pleased with the result. Maggie waited for his praise, in vain, but he had looked impressed.

The warm weather continued but Martina warned her it would probably get cool again soon.

Antonio seemed less prickly than he'd been in the beginning, especially now Maggie was learning Italian. He'd obviously thought her a spoilt brat who'd inherited the villa and wouldn't fit in the village, but she now managed to say hello to the villagers and hoped to get to know them better when her Italian was more fluent.

'How are we getting on with the pool permission?' she asked Antonio one morning when he came to check on progress.

'Good. The man from the commune came and measured up. It has to be more than ten metres away from the road, and many other considerations, but where we have planned it, it is alright,' Antonio answered, with a typical shrug of his shoulders. 'The small pool is no problem either as that is an existing situation. We just need you to accompany me to the commune to sign some paperwork. Perhaps one morning next week?'

'I am not sure I mentioned it, but I would like to have a saltwater pool with steps inside, not a ladder if possible for the big pool.' Maggie told him.

Antonio raised his eyebrows. 'A saltwater pool? It is not usual here in Italy to have such a system. I suppose the pool people will have some knowledge about such things.'

'Well I certainly hope so as I hate chlorine pools. We have many of them in Australia. Perhaps the machinery for the small one could be housed in the adjoining small barn. What about the main one? Will it all go in the existing garden shed?'

'I think it should do. I will get onto the pool people in Perugia and get them to come up and give us some quotes now that we know we can go ahead.'

'The other thing is to enlarge the kitchen as it's poky at the moment,' Maggie added.

Antonio signalled the senior workman over. 'Is your boss coming over sometime soon?' he asked him. The boss, being the builder in charge, came only about once a week. He was a tall red-headed Italian, something Maggie thought unusual; she'd always viewed Italians as dark haired.

He confirmed the boss would be there later in the day so Antonio suggested Maggie return after lunch and they could discuss the matter. He mentioned he needed to be there to translate, as Maggie couldn't speak Italian. She said nothing as she hadn't told him she was learning the language. When she was confident enough she would surprise him, especially seeing she could understand a lot more than she let on.

Chapter Four

Driving back and forth from the hotel to the villa had become tedious, and staying in the hotel, even in the off season, was expensive. Maggie investigated renting a small apartment in the town and arranged to be shown one later in the afternoon. She had to minimise her costs as her money was running out. She had opened a bank account locally where, thankfully, the bank teller spoke English and, even though she had brought in her passport and all the required paperwork, the sole teller took ages, and a huge line had formed.

Later that day when she returned to the villa, she noted a large truck parked there beside Antonio's Peugeot. On entering the courtyard she saw the big red-haired builder in earnest conversation with Antonio. They stopped talking when Maggie appeared.

'We think we can get a simple kitchen in but need to knock a wall down to do so. There is a very good place down near the lake where you can look at kitchens and also it sells light fittings and rugs. It might be a good idea for you to do that,' Antonio told her.

'It will not be too expensive, and I can take away the old one,' the builder added.

Maggie agreed, then said goodbye. Then she drove back into town where the local realtor showed her an extremely small apartment in a small building off the main piazza; it had just two flights of stairs and a car park underneath. The apartment faced the river and had one bedroom, a kitchen, living room and tiny bathroom. A tiny balcony, on which she imagined pots of bright geraniums, was accessed from the living room via French doors, and outside shutters kept out the sun. It was perfect and would be so much easier than driving long distances to the villa each day. She took it on a short term lease, hoping the villa would be ready, and more importantly, the cottage for her to live in before too long. As it was still the low season, the rent was cheap. A quick visit to the local store Antonio had told her about and she had bought all the essentials for the apartment at a very reasonable cost.

At the weekend, Maggie packed up ready to move into the apartment. Sadly she said goodbye to the lovely hotel staff, and also to Geoffrey. One of the old school, he was very much a gentleman. She would miss them all, including the swimming pool.

Geoffrey had told her about a gardening organisation she might be interested in joining, *The Italian Garden Group*, as she was keen on gardening and it would be a way to meet more people. They exchanged addresses as he expected to move back into his own house soon, and he was still keen to see the villa and the restoration being undertaken.

Maggie's Italian lessons were inspiring but the grammar was quite difficult to grasp, and reminded her of Latin at school. However, Italians were forgiving and approved of her efforts. The fact you actually made an effort to speak their language was the main thing, unlike the French who were impatient with mistakes. Maggie found it much easier to practice as she wasn't frightened of using the wrong word or tense; it was such a beautiful language.

Her friends in Australia were good at keeping in touch and were keen to tell her she wasn't missing much in the Sydney winter. They still envied her lifestyle in Italy, probably imagining her lazing on a beach on the Amalfi coast. Like Maggie, no one had much idea where Umbria was. They had all heard of the big cities and the major lakes but none had heard of Lake Trasimeno. She was sure there would be tourist potential here.

She emailed the flat-mates, giving them her new address and then retired to bed, exhausted. She'd had a very busy few days stocking up for the new apartment, but everything would come in handy when she eventually moved into the cottage. She climbed into bed and fell fast asleep.

Church bells clanging noisily nearby woke her the next morning. Then traffic sounds filtered in, car doors being slammed and children's voices chatting on their way to school. She rose and showered; made some breakfast from the produce she had bought at the local supermarkets. While they were well stocked, she still bought her vegetables and fruit in the local market where the camaraderie was wonderful, the locals all greeting each other cheerfully – so different from the supermarkets back home.

Maggie's Italian had been steadily improving though she could understand more than she could speak. Sometimes, however, the villagers spoke in dialect, which made it more difficult. But she tested her new language whenever she could, often greeting the men who congregated in the local cafés, playing cards and drinking espresso, perhaps having a Grappa or two, as she passed.

Today she decided she needed a haircut and popped into the local hairdressers in town. There didn't seem to be an appointment system so Maggie asked in her halting Italian for a haircut and was asked to sit and wait. She would be seen to '*subito*' (soon).

Before long she ushered to a tall, good-looking man, Gaetano, who seemed to be the owner.

'*Non troppo corto*! (not too short)' Maggie said, and smiled at his attempt to respond in English.

On leaving she noticed the beauty salon upstairs specialised in manicures and popped up there to make a booking. The attractive woman Antonio had been with the other day was having her nails done and Maggie's heart sank. This close up she realised just how stunning the young woman was. With her gorgeous dark hair and superb figure, no wonder Antonio wasn't interested in her.

Maggie felt the happiness sink out of her, yet frowned that she should feel that way – she didn't even like Antonio. *Maybe it's just because he's not attracted to me,* she thought.

Although she was loathe to admit it, Antonio was doing an excellent job on the villa. And he had thawed out considerably since their first meeting, making her wonder why he'd been so unfriendly in the beginning.

The villa indeed was coming on amazingly well and once the kitchen was completed, the work on the cottage would begin. The pool company had turned up and said it would be easy to convert the small-disused pool at the cottage to a small plunge pool with saltwater. The main pool would also be built in the 'garden.

The garden couldn't really be described as anything other than grounds as it was such a mess. Maggie had been reading up about plants for Mediterranean climates and had a few quotes from garden designers but they were horrendously expensive. She had drawn up a design of her own and decided to go with that. After all it would be far more appealing to have it just how she wanted and it would be her own special place. She imagined the garden transformed with lavender, roses and a few pencil cypresses trees, plants she had seen at the garden centre not far from the hotel where she had stayed in Tuoro. She just needed the funds to buy them, the thought causing concern.

Next day Maggie called into see Antonio in the office. 'I am really worrying, Antonio. I must get the villa completed soon so I can rent it out. I will shortly run out of money and if the worst happens, and I can't rent it out then I will have to put it on the market.'

'I certainly hope it doesn't come to that. Houses in Italy are not selling quickly at the moment. But the work is coming on well. Don't worry, I will make sure the workmen keep up to schedule. We are lucky we haven't found anything nasty like termites in the woodwork.'

'Well I suppose that makes me feel better,' Maggie said cynically. 'Anyway I've just moved to an apartment in town, so much better than being in the hotel.'

He looked surprised, then nodded that it was a good idea, and went back to sorting through the villa plans on his desktop.

She watched him a moment, noticing not for the first time his intriguingly dark good looks. Her heart skipped a beat then she felt rather foolish – he had a strikingly gorgeous girlfriend and had shown no interest in her romantically. So where had these feelings come from? Perhaps because he hadn't bothered too much with her, it made him all the more desirable.

As he discussed the plans with her, she couldn't take her eyes off his strong, muscular arms; she imagined them holding her and hoped he couldn't read her mind. Then he looked up and his eyes locked with hers for a minute. She didn't say a word but felt something akin to an electric current course through her. Why, when she thought him the most arrogant man she'd ever met, was she feeling this sudden, unbidden attraction?

Chapter Five

The following Sunday Maggie had just settled on her tiny balcony to read a book when her mobile phone started to ring. She picked it up, the voice on the other end sounding familiar. Although she hadn't heard Jonathan's voice for quite a while, she recognised it immediately.

'Hi Maggie. How are you? It's Jonathan here.'

Maggie's heart sank. Why on earth was he calling her and all the way from Australia?

'I'm fine. What's the problem?'

'No problem. I just wanted to catch up with you. It's been a long time.'

Not long enough, Maggie thought, visions of him in bed with the other woman he had dropped her for scooting into her head. She shuddered.

'Is it important for you to ring me from OZ?'

'I'm not ringing you from Australia. Good heavens no. I'm here, sitting in a rental car very close to your apartment according to my Sat Nav.'

Maggie sighed, then felt cold. The last thing she wanted was to see Jonathan again. She had moved on and she was enjoying her single status. He was a bad memory and something she didn't want to think about again. How on earth did he get her address?

'What on earth are you doing here and is that woman with you?'

she asked.

'No, it didn't last. It was all a big mistake. I want to see you and ask your forgiveness. Look, it's all in the past now. I want to tell you I am so sorry about what happened.'

'Well that is beside the point. As you are here, let me know where you are and we can go for a coffee or something.'

She heard him groan. 'I thought you might have a spare room or something seeing I've driven all the way up from Rome.'

'Sorry, I don't have a spare room, but let me know where you are and I will come down.'

Maggie fumed. *What a damned cheek he had!* She certainly wasn't going to let him sleep in her apartment, nor share her bed.

'I'm in a tiny car park off the Piazza Garibaldi, in a rental lease car with red number plates. It's a Renault.'

Maggie gathered her stuff, closed the doors and quickly put on a bit of lipstick, then she picked up her door keys and a sunhat and walked downstairs. She really didn't want to see Jonathan again and thought he had a nerve coming here after the way he'd behaved. She'd worn a pretty lime green sundress today, and felt vibrant, and hoped as she walked that Jonathon might truly regret breaking up with her, given her ego was still bruised by Antonio's disinterest.

She soon found his car, an impatient Jonathan sitting inside drumming his fingers on the steering wheel. She tapped on the window and he jumped out; kissed her on both cheeks.

Maggie recoiled. It was all over between them and she certainly didn't want any physical contact.

'You look so well. Wow, Italy agrees with you!' Jonathan smiled appreciatively at her. Dressed in Polo Ralph Lauren shorts, a T-shirt and docksides, he looked smart, and many women would undoubtedly find him attractive. Maggie had once thought so but his betrayal had put her against him forever. She could never trust him again.

'Well I do love it here but what on earth are you doing turning up like this? You will have to find a room in the local hotel here in town if you really have nowhere to stay. Anyway, we can go and have a coffee or a beer,' and Maggie indicated a nearby café with sun umbrellas up in the piazza.

They wandered to it and Maggie asked Jonathan what he would like. '*Due birre per favore,*' she told the young man behind the bar. Cool beers were just the answer on a hot morning.

'I only have a one bedroom apartment,' Maggie told Jonathan.

His eyes lit up but she shook her head firmly, making it clear he wouldn't be sharing her bed again.

'After what you did I can't believe you can just turn up here like this and expect a bed for the night.' Maggie's grip tightened around her glass. 'You have a hide like a rhinoceros.'

'Well,' Jonathan squirmed, 'it really was nothing. Liz didn't mean anything to me. She had come onto me pretty strong and one thing just led to another. Nothing serious.'

Maggie's lips pursed. Whether it was a one-night stand or not, he had let her down badly and that was the end of it. There was no turning back. Loyalty meant everything to her and she realised she felt nothing for Jonathan as she sat watching him in the sunlight.

'How long are you staying in the area, or are you on your way to somewhere else?' she asked.

'Well I thought I would spend some time with you. However, you are being remarkably unfriendly to a fellow Aussie away from home.'

'I'm sorry you feel like that, but …'; she shrugged. 'I've moved on now. Life in Italy is busy and I'm up to my eyes restoring my aunt's villa.'

Jonathan had obviously heard about the villa from mutual friends and she presumed he'd imagined himself lying in the sun by a pool, being waited on, and forgiven, by a loving Maggie. That it was not going to happen really jolted him.

'Well if that's how you feel! I thought bygones would be bygones and we could pick up the pieces.'

'No, Jonathan, that's never going to happen. However, if you are staying around a while I'll show you the villa and we can just remain friends.'

Disgruntled, Jonathan agreed, and Maggie suggested a hotel in the town where he could stay.

'Meet up with me there for dinner?'

Maggie shook her head. 'It's Sunday. Sunday night is not a good night to go out in Italy. Most people have had a big family Sunday lunch and the restaurants normally close in the evenings after that. Why not come to my apartment and I'll cook – it's just around the corner. Here's the address.'

Jonathan logged it in his mobile phone as well as the name of the hotel. Maggie wasn't sure of its whereabouts exactly but gave him the approximate location. They finished their beers and he arranged to be at her apartment around 7 pm that evening.

She watched him saunter off to his car, knowing he would find someone else very soon as he liked to have a woman around at all times. She picked up her sunglasses and walked home to settle again with her book and cook the evening meal.

The church clock tower chimed seven o'clock just as her doorbell rang: Jonathan, as usual, dead on time. In Italy, time was a more fluid arrangement as she'd found out, a bit like the Irish idea of time, she remembered from past holidays there. Italians were so charming though that anything was forgiven, even being late for appointments.

Maggie had laid a small table for two with a pretty cloth she had bought in the local market, and she had cooked a delicious lasagne. Jonathan turned up with a bottle of red wine. '*Montepulciano,*' she noted with pleasure. It would go well with the lasagne. For dessert she had fresh figs with mascarpone. Fresh ingredients were so important in Italy and meals didn't need to be fussy. She loved the smell of local tomatoes and was amazed to see them growing in low clusters in the fields and not climbing up vines as at home.

Jonathan settled on the sofa and flicked through an out of date magazine she had found at a market stall.

'What happened to the girl with the latest magazines in Sydney?' he asked. 'This magazine is at least a year old!'

'I'm lucky to find anything in English. This is not a big city, Jonathan. I'm living in rural Italy.' She started serving the meal, turned the conversation away from what she used to be like. 'There's a special stall in the market that's run by a charity for homeless dogs. Italians don't feel the same about animals as we do and often get rid of one that's past its 'use by' date for hunting. The charity is run by some rather eccentric English women and is one of the few places that sells English books and magazines.'

'What do the locals hunt?' Jonathan asked.

'Wild boar and truffles mainly. You get both around here. A good truffle-hunting dog is worth a lot of money. Anyway, the lasagne is ready so come and eat.'

Jonathan poured out the wine. In Australia Maggie had always enjoyed Sauvignon Blanc or a Semillon but here she had discovered the wonderful red wines from Montepulciano. It was a coincidence that Jonathan chose one of those.

After they'd eaten, Maggie poured out a glass of Limoncello from the fridge.

'That was terrific. I'm sorry we parted before on such bad terms,' Jonathan said, looking guilty.

Maggie shrugged. 'It's all in the past. If you like, I'll show you the villa tomorrow – you can either meet me here or up at the villa. It's about 5 kilometres up in the hills.'

'Well, shall I meet you here about 10 o'clock? I thought I might just stay a couple of days at the hotel here then move on up to Florence.'

Maggie sighed. Jonathan had thankfully realised she had no interest in resurrecting their relationship. Before leaving though he had kissed her passionately but she did not respond to it, and he shrugged dejectedly and said he would see her in the morning. Maggie wasn't sorry to see him go – he was part of her past.

The following morning, standing on her doorstep, Jonathan agreed to follow her up to the villa in his lease car, Maggie suggesting they meet up on the road outside of town after clearing traffic, where she would wait for him in a layby. He tooted at her little red Fiat then drove behind her under the railway line and up into the hills. She indicated early for the turn off to the villa and they parked beneath the trees.

Antonio wasn't there but the builders remained busy re-pointing the stonework on the cottage. The villa was almost finished, and the pool people were due the next day to commence digging the foundations. The cheerful Neapolitan men smiled knowingly when Maggie turned up with a man in tow. That was definitely something Italians understood. *Amore!* Love!

'Buongiorno,' Maggie called to them.

Jonathan nodded silently as he followed her, his gaze casting round to take it all in. The new IKEA kitchen had now been installed – white cupboards with burnished metal knobs and an Italian range cooker stood in place of the gas hob. Maggie had wanted induction to avoid the electricity problems in the area. The gas, which would be stored in a huge *bombola* in the garden, would also run the central heating. Next to the cooker stood a huge American style fridge/freezer, a dishwasher, and on the bench top a capsule coffee maker.

Painters were due to start work on the walls in a couple of days.

She pointed out the new wall tiles, which were rough-hewn and a delightful contrast to the Caesar-stone worktops, and the Travertine floor, chosen because there wasn't enough of the old bricks to match the living room floors. She led Jonathon through to the laundry room where a washing machine and separate dryer stood. She would rarely use the dryer, electricity being so expensive in Italy, and she knew, with only 6 kw, just using a hairdryer at the same time could trip the fuses.

Letting the house to guests would be a problem, especially with energy guzzling Americans who used dryers all the time. She'd once heard an American woman say she wouldn't line-dry in case her neighbours thought she couldn't afford to use a dryer! Maggie had reeled: everyone used clothes lines in Australia. *There's nothing so delightful as slipping between sheets that dried in the open air.*

'Electricity can be a huge problem here,' she told Jonathan. 'We only have 6 kilowatts and most Italians only have 3. Electricity is so expensive some of the villagers move down to an apartment in town in the winter as they can't afford to heat their stone houses. Did you notice the enormous piles of logs outside all the houses. They're getting ready for winter – that's for their wood stoves so they don't have to use central heating. It's only very recently that they've begun to buy toasters and mixers.'

Maggie took him up the beautiful wide stone staircase to the next floor and showed him the bedrooms, all now finished and attractively furnished, thanks to the Gran Casa emporium. The beds, with delicately carved iron bedheads, were much higher than in Australia. They were already made up with snowy white Italian cotton sheets, with fluffy towels folded on the ends of each bed. Iron bedside tables with glass tops sat beside each bed topped with small bedside lamps that resembled metal tulips. The bathrooms had bidets and walk in showers that were now fully tiled.

Maggie had hung some *Deruta* pottery plates to make a feature wall.

Jonathan's jaw dropped when he saw the enormous upstairs living room with its stunning old beams and inglenook fireplace along one wall. Floor length windows, which thankfully had been put in years ago as nowadays they wouldn't be allowed, bolstered the view. They were all timber joinery with outside shutters. She had hung slim, plain cream, readymade curtains from IKEA at all the windows, tied with luxurious thick gold cord ties.

'This is amazing,' Jonathon said. 'If this was in Sydney it would be mega-bucks. Just think of the wonderful parties you could have in here!'

'Not something I envisage doing,' she shook her head. 'The handful of people I know would look lost in here. Anyway, when I rent out the villa I'm sure it'll be a great attraction.'

'How are you getting on with that?'

'Nowhere at the moment. I have to wait till the pool is built and then take some photos, or get a professional to do it. I'm already working on a website but am stuck until the place looks more habitable.'

'So will you stay here or come back to Sydney?'

'I'm not sure. The truth of it is I'm beginning to enjoy the Italian way of life, but I'm running out of money. I'm not sure this work will be finished before I do … If it isn't I might have to sell up.' She sighed. 'And that would be such as shame because house prices dropped like stones recently.'

'So what else do you have to do here?'

They wandered through the room and out to the terrace 'I still need outdoor furniture and garden umbrellas out here. It's been pretty full on buying furniture and bedding. Luckily I met some English people who showed me where I could buy things at a very reasonable price. They've been terribly helpful.'

Maggie showed him where the pool was going. 'We've had quite a few problems with the pool area. There were some big boulders over there and an old olive tree we had to move. Then the Government brought in strict new laws regarding earthquake-proofing buildings, including swimming pools. Just what I didn't need! The builders had to hire mini bulldozers which all costs more, of course.'

Pointing to where the grass and weeds stood waist high, Maggie said, 'This is where the old olive tree was that I had to get moved, right where the pool was going to be. It's been replanted over there near the hedge. We had to cover the root ball and replant it in exactly the same orientation. I just have to make sure I keep watering it so it survives. The grass will be scythed next week and then the pool people will come and do their job.'

Jonathan wandered around admiring the other old, gnarled olive trees.

'They're at least 500 years old,' she told him, causing his eyes to widen. 'Would you like a coffee, Jonathan?'

She indicated a chair under the rickety terrace pergola which she planned to cover in wisteria.

Jonathan perched on a chair. 'You certainly do need some decent outdoor furniture.'

'I know. It's all a question of priorities at the moment. I'll go and make the coffees, and some for the workmen too, so it may take a while. Just sit and relax and enjoy the view.'

Thankfully she'd bought some pods for the new capsule maker and set the *moka* coffee pot on the stove for the Italians. They loved their coffee strong and ridiculously sweet.

While waiting for it to brew, she scanned the estimate for the pool again. It was much higher than she'd expected and money was getting tight. But it was impossible to rent a house in the summer in Italy without one, and until the pool was finished she couldn't take photos to put on the web. The worries came churning back.

Carrying out the coffee and some Amaretto biscuits to the terrace, she noted Jonathan had indeed made himself at home, propping his feet up on the table and enjoying the sunshine. She only had a few tatty director's chairs and buying new ones was another added expense. She returned to the kitchen and took the workers' coffee out to the rear terrace.

"Grazie, Signora' they enthused when they saw a plate of Amaretto biscuits for them too.

When she returned to sit opposite Jonathan, the warm sun's rays basking her face, he asked, 'How long do you think you will stay here then?'

'I'm in no hurry. I want to get this all up and running and ready to rent for next season. I'll be living in the cottage hopefully by then and can keep it warm and snug in the winter.'

'Well I think it's a huge undertaking and what sort of life are you going to have out here? You will end up a bitter and twisted old maid if you don't get a life for yourself.'

Maggie snorted. 'Good heavens, Umbria's not the end of the world you know! And I'm going to join an Italian Garden Group I've heard about, and will meet more people that way.'

He grimaced. 'Oh well, it's your life. Sounds like lots of dotty people wandering around in straw hats, and they're probably ancient too.' Then he changed the subject. 'I'm heading off to Florence in the morning. Will you have dinner with me at the hotel tonight before I go?'

 'Yes, alright. I've heard the food is good there.'

He nodded appreciatively. 'And you can't just live here and not come back to Australia where all your friends are. You need to get a life, Maggie!'

"Stop worrying about my life! And I'm too busy here to think about anything else at the moment. This restoration work will keep me occupied for ages.'

The sound of a car driving up the road meant someone was coming to the villa, there being no other dwelling past the end of the lane. Sure enough, Antonio had come to check on the builders. The dogs of course started barking. He strode through the gateway and halted, his eyebrows rising when he saw Jonathan.

'Ciao, I am sorry, I didn't realise you had company. I hope I am not intruding.'

Jonathan's jaw tightened and his gaze hardened as he scanned the Italian top to toe. Maggie sensed his angst.

'Antonio, of course you are not. Please, meet my friend Jonathan from Sydney. He's staying in the area for a couple of days. Jonathan, this is Antonio who oversees all the work here. His advice is invaluable.'

Jonathan stood up and shook Antonio's hand, and Maggie could see him sizing up the tall, good looking Italian, adding up two and two and making three. The air bristled with tension between the two men.

'Sorry to say goodbye so soon but I was just leaving. Maggie, I will expect you around 7 tonight?' He put his empty coffee cup on the table and sauntered off through the doorway, his annoyance that the Italian was friendly with Maggie obvious.

Maggie sighed with relief that he was going. She had heaps to do and didn't want to babysit Jonathan during his whole visit to Umbria. He had little idea of history and no interest in Roman artefacts so Italy was rather lost on him. She knew darned well he'd come to check out the villa, and probably thought he would get around her easily. No doubt he had expected her aunt would have left a considerable amount of money. Jonathan liked the good things in life without actually wanting to work too hard to obtain them. She was also quite happy he had got the wrong impression about Antonio. It wouldn't hurt him to be sidelined. If only he knew that she and Antonio could barely be civil to each other!

'Antonio, would you like a coffee?'

'No thank you. I had one just before leaving the studio.'

Maggie smiled. Italians tended to limit their coffee drinking and also never had milky coffee after lunch. They were very careful of their digestive systems, which she found quite amusing.

Antonio wanted to talk to her about the disturbing news about the pool. Because of the earthquake risk and the fact it was on a hill, the foundations had to be dug very deep and it had to be reinforced. It was all going to be more expensive than first thought. He'd spoken to the builder who was bringing in extra machinery to undertake the work

'I am sorry about this, but they have just brought in these new laws since the big earthquake in Assisi. Typically, of course, it has taken a long time to enact these and unfortunately for you, they have just been put into law.'

Maggie shrugged. There was nothing she could do, unless she could go out and get a job to help tide things over. She shook her head, and frowned.

Antonio also frowned, and eventually said, 'Was that your boyfriend who just left?'

'A very definite ex-boyfriend,' she smiled. 'He just turned up out of the blue.'

'Out of the blue?' Antonio queried, not understanding slang terms.

She smiled wider. 'We broke up ages ago and he thought he could just come here and all would be ok again, that he could stay with me.'

Antonio looked confused. Then he turned to speak to one of the workmen who had come with a query. Maggie wondered if the attractive woman she'd seen Antonio with was his regular girlfriend. She didn't feel she could ask him, despite his questioning her just now. Anyway it was more important to talk about money and the work in progress. If they didn't finish soon she would miss the summer season and there was no way she could afford to do that. She would concentrate on the main villa and just do less expensive work on the cottage; she just had to make it livable so she wasn't paying rent. If the villa wasn't rented out, she couldn't carry on and would have to take a loss and sell up and that was a much bigger problem at the moment.

Jonathan was waiting for her in the hotel bar later that evening. 'What would you like to drink?' he asked as she perched on a high stool next to him.

'Campari and orange, thanks.' It was her preferred choice these days.

'Nice outfit. You certainly seem to be fitting in to the Italian lifestyle wearing dresses rather than trousers.'

Maggie smiled. She'd chosen to wear another linen sundress, a bright pink one she'd bought in the local market. The dresses had been so ridiculously cheap she'd tried some on in the van beside the stall, the local women giggling as she'd paraded each one in the open doorway. Once she'd found her size, she knew she could simply buy another one the following week without trying it on and this way she was creating quite a good wardrobe for the summer.

They wandered out to their table on the terrace.

'So what are your plans now, Jonathan?' Maggie asked as she sat down.

'I'm driving up to Florence. An English guy who's staying here said the traffic is a nightmare there and the motorways are confusing so I've bought a Sat Nav. I'm also going to stop at a popular shopping mall he recommended ... a place called *The Mall*. It's a couple of hours before you reach Florence. The shops are out in the open, not like our shopping malls back home.'

'I like the sound of that. I could do with some new shoes and I just love Italian ones. They're so much cheaper here in Italy ... but,' she shrugged, 'I'll have to earn some money first.'

'Well when you do, you turn off the autrostrada at a little place called Incisa. The shopping centre is well signposted, or you can look it up on the Internet.' He picked up the menu. 'Have you been to Florence yourself yet, or explored the area around here?'

'Not yet. I haven't had the time but I thought I'd take a look at Assisi soon as it's not too far away.' *When I have the money,* she added internally. '

'What did I tell you about not getting around? Anyway, what's with the Italian Lothario?'

Maggie knew sooner or later Jonathan would shoot his barb about Antonio. She wasn't about to let on it was a purely professional relationship, frigid at times – certainly not amorous! But it was just desserts if Jonathan thought they were in a relationship.

'Oh, he's just the geometra overseeing the restoration work. So after Florence, what are your plans?' she swiftly changed the subject.

'I thought I'd wander over to the Ligurian coast as its not far, taking in Pisa on the way.'

'Oh how lovely. I am missing the sea. I would love to explore all those lovely areas, in particular Portofino. There's so much to see and do in Italy. Pompeii, Herculaneum, the Amalfi Coast …'

They chatted amicably while lingering over their food. But eventually it was time for Maggie leave. They hugged; kissed platonically and vowed to remain friends. Jonathan couldn't resist pointing out how unfaithful Italian men were, which she thought was hypocritical seeing he had betrayed her.

Jonathan stood and watched as Maggie roared off in the little red Fiat, and sighed. *Oh well, An end to an era,* he thought, and sighed again. *But, there's fun to be had in Florence and definitely in Portofino.*

His smile lengthened at the thought of all those fantastic yachts moored there, which were bound to have lots of bikini-clad women on board. He thought Maggie a fool for being involved with an Italian man, sensing there was more to the relationship than she admitted. Obviously though, it would never lead anywhere. She would come to her senses one day but by then he would have moved on.

Chapter Six

Over the next few weeks, the pool at the villa began to take shape. The company brought in the small diggers required and created an enormous hole, which they lined with stainless steel panels to form a box. This was the expensive part and the workmen toiled in the heat, shirtless and hatless, their skin glistening in the sun – so unlike Australia's slip, slop and slap, long sleeve shirts and work helmets.

The pool was soon ready for the pool liner. Maggie perused the colour charts and chose a sand colour, which meant the pool water would be a translucent greenish-blue colour. She hated the sight of bright blue pools in the countryside and thought them incongruous. After the liner was painstakingly fitted, the water tanker arrived and water flowed from a hosepipe, filling it quickly. The pool equipment was housed in a small dark green shed near the end of the garden, hidden from sight.

'I love it, Antonio,' Maggie gushed.

'Yes, it is looking good but now you need to find something to go around the pool. It has to wait for a week or two, till things settle down so they will put gravel there for now. I would suggest you go to the tile shop where you found the kitchen tiles and see what they have. It needs to be frost-proof and not slippery.'

Maggie did as he suggested and chose beautiful brick-type tiles that didn't scream 'new', with a slightly rough feel, and they weren't hideously expensive.

The steps down into the pool were so much easier to walk down than a ladder, and Maggie knew she would enjoy sitting on the steps, her feet in the water and a glass of Prosecco or Campari in her hand. At the wonderful Gran Casa store she had bought some plastic glasses as friends in Sydney had broken a glass in their pool and had to employ a diver at great expense to collect all the shards on the bottom. She had decided against the electronic pool cover as the cost was too high but they had made provision for one so it could be installed at a later date. At the moment, money was the overriding factor in all decisions.

The cottage was almost finished and was plain and simple, keeping the costs down. The small plunge pool was also ready to use and the equipment for that hidden in what had been an old barn. The cottage was built around three sides so was private and sheltered but the area around it was pretty wild and needed landscaping. Maggie worried there might be snakes there as one of the workmen had recently pointed out a viper slithering down the wall. Living in Sydney snakes were rarely seen and Maggie was terrified of them. She therefore bought a trimmer to keep the weeds down.

The Membership Secretary of the Italian branch of The Garden Group rang one day and explained how to join. She told Maggie all about the next meeting which would be held in some beautiful gardens near Florence (*Firenze* as it was called in Italy). The meetings were often held in Italian, although strangely enough almost every member was either English or German. The secretary said they were going to stay overnight in a hotel in the hills near Fiesole, which sounded wonderful so Maggie asked to be included. She needed a break to take her mind off the villa and the money problems, which were getting her down and robbing her of sleep.

Later that day, she wandered around town, and bought some terracotta pots for the terrace, marked down in a sale. She also found someone to tackle the garden for her. He was Moroccan and spoke mostly Italian but knew a little English. She had also taken the advice of the English couple she'd met and bought some discounted wrought iron chairs to go around the outside table. The pergola was another problem: she managed to explain to the gardener that she wanted the bamboo removed to allow the wisteria and anything else she planted there to cover it. When it came down, floods of dried leaves, scorpions and caterpillars emerged, making a filthy, choking mess. However, once removed, it looked splendid.

Now that Maggie had learnt some Italian she decided to engage with the local villagers. Before her lessons, she'd said hello and kept walking, worried they would try to engage in conversation. Recently she'd gained the confidence to talk to them about the restoration and the garden. One of the villagers had kindly given her some eggs from her own chickens, and had also given her the name of a young woman, Francesca, who lived opposite the castle. Francesca spoke English, so Maggie decided to call on her.

A handsome young boy answered the door and called out to his mother. Welcoming her inside, she obviously guessed who Maggie was and brought out some cold drinks. Maggie talked to her about the plans for the villa and her need for some help there, and wondered if she knew anyone who would come in to clean.

Francesca thought about it for a few minutes and then said she had someone in mind and this woman lived at the other end of the village.

'If you like I will ask this person and then if she says yes, we can arrange a meeting.'

'Thank you so much. I would be very grateful. I was wondering about the people who live in the village and also who owns the castle opposite here?'

'A young couple recently bought it and are busy organising restoration work. It is a huge undertaking as the *castello* is about 800 years old. I'm sure they would like to meet you so you should call in to see them next time they are here. They live in England somewhere and spend holidays here in Umbria but will be here next weekend I know. As for the villagers, there is a widow near your house who keeps chickens, a retired farmer, and also a man on his own whose wife has left him. Sadly the bar closed some time ago as that was very busy and we also once had a shop too.'

'I have met the lovely old lady who gave me some eggs and she told me about you,' Maggie replied.

When Francesca spoke about the village, Maggie was awed at the how casually Francesca spoke about the castle – about 800 years old! – so very different from Australia where, apart from the Aborigines who had lived there for thousands of years, Europeans hadn't even discovered Australia yet.

As she sipped her cool drink, she looked down the hill at the sprawling green countryside below, and the small cottages dotted around the hills opposite. Francesca told her that in the autumn hunters would roam the hills and woods truffle hunting. It was dangerous to go walking through the woods then. There were also wild boars to be aware of. Maggie could hear dogs barking; it seemed that everywhere around dogs were barking.

'I was a bit worried about some of the dogs in the village. They don't look very well cared for,' Maggie told Francesca.

'Oh I know which ones you mean. The owner is quite mean and he beats them. The vet could take a look at the kennels but it is difficult to make a complaint about them. The owner is very friendly with the *carabinieri* officer in the station in town. This man is also a very unpleasant person. It might mean a lot of trouble if you did anything. There is something called *a Denunzia* and the person complaining is supposed to be a secret. However, this person knowing the *carabinieri* like he does, it would be no secret. It is better to not do anything I am sorry to say.'

Maggie felt quite sad at this. In Australia she would just ring up the ranger, or animal welfare and it would be looked into. She wondered quietly if she still could do something as it disturbed her to see the poor animals cowed and frightened. She had an idea and thought she would talk to the dog stall people at the market. They would be bound to know what to do.

She also asked Francesca if she knew if it was possible to get a job teaching English to Italians. Francesca promised to find out from someone she knew, who did similar.

The following day Maggie visited the plant centre again and chose plants for the new garden. The irrigation system had been installed which would drip feed water to the plants, and the paths and pool surround were now finished.

She chose her favourites: *Hidcote* lavender; prostrate rosemary, which would hang down and soften the walls around the pool, agapanthus and box hedging. She also bought dozens of rose bushes, which had to be ordered from the wholesale rose growers further north, between Lucca and Pisa where the most enormous fields of roses grew, as well as fields of mature *Iceberg, Sally Holmes* and other cream and white varieties on her list. She also chose *Sea Foam* then she couldn't resist a few glorious climbing roses to go over the garage at the rear of the villa. Finally she picked out some oleanders to go at the end of the garden and also by the shed near the pool. They had poisonous leaves but she just loved oleanders, and they didn't mind the dry climate.

As she added four pencil shaped cypress trees to her list, she was glad she'd decided to oversee the whole garden project herself. She could already see the grand effect each plant would have on the garden.

The Garden Group meeting and visit to Fiesole was soon

coming up and Maggie looked forward to the social activity.

Helen, one of the older group members, rang her one day and suggested they meet for coffee in her favourite downtown café, so next morning, instead of heading up to the villa, Maggie parked the little Fiat under the trees and walked across the road to the café. She found a table by the window and waited until someone unmistakably English arrived. Eventually a very harassed-looking woman appeared clutching a straw hat to her head. Maggie recognised her as she'd often seen this woman at the dog charity stall. They greeted each other and Helen insisted on buying their coffees. She then proceeded to talk to Maggie almost non-stop, about life in Italy, about the dreadful dog problems, and finally the Garden Group and the visit to Fiesole. The party was booked into a small local hotel and if Maggie would like a lift, that could be arranged.

'That would be a great idea. I have no idea where places are, as I have been so busy sorting out the villa I haven't really been anywhere yet. I am also terrified of Italian driving! I hope to buy myself a car as I'm still renting the one I drive and it's getting expensive.'

They discussed the gardens and somehow the conversation turned to the last war when the Italians had been very short of food. So many older people had suffered from rickets, evident by their misshapen bowed legs, and the villagers had become used to making do with very little. She had seen some of them foraging for what looked to be weeds.

'If you go across the lake there is a small village called Gioiella, and the small *alimentare* there, you know the grocery shop, has bullet marks all over the walls still from the war and they will never remove them as a reminder what the Germans did to them. They lined up the men in the village and machine-gunned them to death.' Helen shuddered as she recounted the event. 'Anyway let us think about gardens and beautiful things now and forget about the past.'

Seeing her husband, George, was back in Suffolk visiting his elderly mother, Helen offered to pick Maggie up on the morning of the field trip. 'You'll meet George when he gets back,' she added as she scooped up her hat and basket. 'You must come up and have lunch with us one day. Talk to you soon.' Then she rushed off, leaving Maggie feeling somewhat breathless for the chat, eager to visit the beautiful hilltop village of Montone where Helen lived, and appreciative that she had learnt so much that morning in such a short time.

Maggie suddenly remembered that, in about a week's time, it was her best friend's birthday in Sydney so she drove into town, visited a card shop and riffled through the offerings to find one suitable. Of course the words were in Italian but she thought that would make it more exotic. Hastily, she wrote a few words in it and copied down the address from her mobile phone. Then she asked directions to the Post Office, the only place she could buy overseas stamps.

When she walked in to the building, it looked horrendously busy, people sitting or standing around waiting to be served. She found a machine by the door, which she punched with the service she required and removed the paper ticket. Number 18. With everything written in Italian, she hoped she had picked the right service. *Heavens,* she wondered, *how long will I have to wait?*

People obviously obtained their pensions in this long-winded manner and clerks at the desk enthusiastically stamped forms. Bureaucracy certainly wasn't dead here. In future she would bring a book with her and just settle down and wait.

Eventually she reached the clerk who weighed the card and stamped it. She was free for the rest of the day, and, as she had never been to Assisi, she decided at that moment to drive there. It wasn't too far , not much further than Perugia airport. In fact, the beautiful town could be seen from the airport itself.

As she drove uphill towards Assissi, the town spread out in all its glory and she was awed that only a few years ago it had suffered the devastating earthquake Geoffrey had told her about. Parking in a large car park, she followed the small crowd up an outdoor escalator into the town itself, strode past cafes and the beautiful The Temple of Minerva,. She smiled pleasantly at the priest sitting outside, and couldn't resist stopping to view the interior. It was highly decorated in gold and was very ornate. It might have started off as a temple but was now very much a stunning Roman Catholic Church. A couple of nuns walked in, made the sign of the cross with the Holy water and genuflected in front of the altar. Maggie knelt down and said a prayer for her aunt, for without her she wouldn't be visiting this beautiful town. She also prayed that she would get the restoration done soon and be able to rent out the villa. She certainly felt like some help from above. She lit a candle and hoped fervently that would bring her good luck.

When she left the church, she wandered along the ancient road towards the amazing basilica of St. Francis at the end, which dominated the town like a sentinel overlooking the surrounding countryside. Down below, hordes of tourists milled around amongst black-frocked priests and nuns. The order of St Francis, the Franciscans, were in abundance too, dressed in long brown simple habits as St. Francis had been all those centuries ago.

She walked into the basilica and an appreciative sigh escaped her as she took in the blue Lapis Lazuli ceilings and frescoes, as the sound of a mass being sung reached her ears. Every so often a religious man hissed at the crowd of tourists '*Silenzio*' insisting they remain silent in this place of worship. However, it was difficult not to converse with their companions with so much to admire, so there was a constant hum of sounds emanating from the tourists. As she drew near the altar, she could see and hear the choir taking part in the service, and tears came to her eyes – it was so incredibly moving. She followed the crowd down the steps to the crypt below to visit the tomb of St. Francis, and mingled with them in the heat and claustrophobic atmosphere of the chapel. She couldn't wait to get out, as to be in such a crush was frightening. She felt relief climbing the steps again into fresh air.

Wanting to avoid more crowds, Maggie decided to go, glad though that she had come and seen a place that was more beautiful than she had imagined. There were shops selling lace mantillas, T shirts, souvenirs and even pretty lace fans. She bought one of the latter as well as a few postcards to send home. They even sold airmail stamps. Pausing at a shop selling gelatos, she treated herself to one and ate it on her way back to the car park.

One place ticked off my list, she thought, *and not long till I go to Fiesole.* Maggie looked forward to that enormously, especially as she would meet some more English-speaking people. She had begun to miss the social life. However, she didn't want to mix exclusively with ex-pats as she wanted to get to know more Italians, which was proving difficult. At least she'd made one friend locally, in the house opposite the castle. She guessed she really ought to introduce herself to the castello people too. Finding a job to help out the finances was also a priority.

The thought of returning to Australia unsettled her and she realised how much Italy meant to her. Annoyingly, Antonio too, but that was a ridiculous situation. How on earth had he crept under her radar when he'd given her no encouragement?

Parking the little Fiat under a shady tree, Maggie walked up to the apartment. A shower and a cool drink were next on the list. As she put the key in her door, she noticed her neighbour opposite hovering around. '*Buonasera!*' she greeted her with pleasure. '*Parla Italiano?*' she asked Maggie.

'*Me scusi io parla Italiano un poco*' she replied, saying she hoped in the correct Italian, that she only spoke a little of the language. However, she wasn't sure if she'd mixed up the grammar. The old lady smiled and asked her to come in for a cold drink.

Maggie didn't like to refuse, even though she was dying for a shower and to put her feet up. She followed the lady in to her dark abode, Italians liking to keep the shutters closed to keep out the heat. Lace doilies and what her mother had called 'anti-macassars' were draped on all the chairs, and ornaments and photos of, presumably, children and grandchildren cluttered every surface. Religious pictures and a huge crucifix decorated the walls

The woman gestured to Maggie to sit on the rather hard looking sofa while she busied herself in the kitchen pouring out cold drinks for them both. There was nothing comfortable in the apartment, Maggie noticed, recalling how Italians in general sat on hard kitchen chairs; how they didn't own comfortable furniture, and she wondered if life had been tough for them over the years.

Maggie spent as much time as she could with her neighbour, Signora Ada, and promised to return another day. She let herself into her apartment, threw off her shoes and headed for the shower.

Her mobile phone beeped as she was towelling herself dry: she had missed a call from Antonio. She'd not been in touch with the geometra for days so immediately worried there were problems with the cottage. She rang him back, that familiar impression that he thought her a spoilt young woman, who'd been indulged by a wealthy aunt seeping back in. He did not of course know that she had always worked hard for a living, up until now.

'Ciao, Maggie.' He sounded terse. 'I wondered if you were coming up to see the villa and cottage tomorrow?'

'Si, Antonio. I am definitely coming up.' She couldn't resist telling him about her time in Assisi and how wonderful it was. 'I also need to buy a car to replace the rental I have. Do you know somewhere I can get a good deal? Renting is just too expensive.'

'Sure. I know someone in the town. I will take you down to meet him.'

He sounded more friendly, and pleased she had enjoyed Assisi. They arranged to meet up at 10 am the next day and he assured her there were no problems, just decisions to be made. 'Not having a rental car will cut your costs considerably, and you can always sell the new car on when you leave,' he added.

She noted that remark – he seemed totally convinced she wouldn't stay.

As she drove up to the village, Maggie decided she would to call in on the couple who lived at the huge, forboding castle that towered above the road. She wasn't sure however how one approached the entrance. Never mind, she would ask Antonio – he would probably know.

When she arrived at the cottage, Antonio was already there. He smiled at her and showed her the tiles they had chosen, which looked wonderful now they were in place. The cottage was coming together beautifully. A large wood-burning stove had been placed in the living room and the dark wooden beams were lime-washed and reminded her of houses she'd seen in France. The kitchen, although small, was well planned with a wall oven and a stone sink similar to a Belfast sink. The tapware was very smart, and there was a large fridge/freezer with icemaker. She was pleased to see plenty of power points and the ceiling fans she'd ordered were in place. The bathroom had a large walk-in shower, a loo and of course a bidet. She had asked Antonio to source a bath for her as on cold nights she enjoyed soaking in a hot, deep bath and listening to music. The wall tiles were white but had a slim blue and white feature tile all around the wall, which looked stunning. The Italian tiles she had used would cost a fortune in Sydney.

In the distance she could hear those darned, barking dogs going off again. They were beginning to annoy her.

Antonio checked some fixtures then came across to her. 'Come. I want to show you the plunge pool. It will be the same colour as the main pool but with a ladder.'

'No, I want steps,' Maggie corrected.

'Steps will make the pool very small. A ladder takes up less space.'

'No, I hate ladders! I don't mind how small the pool is and I can just cool off in it and sit on the steps.'

'*Bene*. Ok, then you have it your way!' Antonio grinned at her.

'*Allora*, that's fine.'

'Oh, I see you are picking up some Italian!' he laughed.

'Hmm. Yes, well I am taking the lessons you suggested, but I do laugh … you Italians always have the last word. When I say thank you for something, you all say '*Prego*' back!'

Laughing, he touched her on the shoulder, which sent a shiver through her, and guided her into the cottage.

The cottage had a central heating system but she doubted she would use it: electricity was so expensive. The wood-burning stove would suffice. They had installed solar panels in the roof, which had to be put out of sight, as it was a conservation area. There were solar panels on the garage roof too, which heated the pool. That would be useful in the summer and autumn and stretch out the swimming period by at least another month, she hoped. It was important to let the villa out for as long as possible.

'I have to get back to my office before lunch but would you like to join me for coffee in town now?' Antonio said.

Maggie's eyebrow rose. That was unusual; she'd often felt he avoided having anything personal to do with her, but inwardly her heart leapt as she nodded.

They arranged to meet in a café near the big supermarket and lingered over coffee and *cornetto,* the equivalent of a French croissant, while Antonio talked about his family and how he had learnt English at school, and taken a few holiday jobs in the UK, so he spoke English well … and, of course, his mother was English. He seemed able to flit from one language to the other with ease. Then Maggie told him about her lack of family and how important her aunt had been to her since her parents died. It was obvious Antonio had been impressed with her aunt. She was very eccentric but such a feisty lady and didn't want to spoil a beautiful old building with unattractive modern features. This alone endeared her to him.

'I am worried about the pool being finished in time for photos to be taken. I need to get the villa on the website as soon as possible so I can start renting it out.'

'It won't be much longer. A clever photographer can take the house and pool from the right angles if everything isn't quite finished. If you don't know anyone, I can find someone for you. We can get that organised next week if you like.'

'Francesca knows someone so I think I can get it organised. I'm just so worried about missing the summer season.

'And I hate those barking dogs in the village. They look malnourished and mistreated and I fear paying guests will be put off if they are mentioned on *Trip Advisor* – that could be a real problem.'

'Those are hunting dogs – not many dogs in Italy are household pets. However, the man who owns them is not a pleasant man and you would be wise to keep out of any trouble there. You could have a word with the man's sister who lives there.'

Maggie grimaced. She hated seeing, or even hearing of, animals being mistreated. The thought of it occurring grated on her and she knew she wouldn't let it rest.

'Do you want to meet the guy who sells cars and see if he can find what you would like?'

'What a good idea. I wouldn't mind having a little Fiat like I have now. It's so easy to drive and great on the narrow roads in the town. Cost is the main thing – I don't have much cash left.

'I am sorry about that. The problem with the big boulders took much longer to get the pool dug. And of course it had to be earthquake proof. There is always an element of danger when a structure is built on the side of a hill. I know the cost will be greater than expected, but there was nothing I could do.'

Maggie's heart sank. So close to finishing and she was running out of cash. What she needed was a job, but what could she do with her limited Italian. She hoped Francesca would come up with something.

Antonio led the way to the garage, which was close by. When they walked onto the forecourt, Maggie spied another Fiat like her rental, but with a sunroof; she immediately decided it would be her car, if the price was right. It was also bright red. Antonio introduced her to the owner, who showed her a couple of other cars, but her gaze kept returning to the red one. Antonio left her to discuss the details and to returned to his office, Maggie advising him before he left that she was going to Fiesole for a few days.

She hoped to get the car all sorted out before then – the price was good and, after filling in a few forms and submitting her credit card, she became the owner of a new (second-hand!) car. Sad that she couldn't take it straight away, she left it there until she returned from Fiesole.

Driving back up the hill, she reached the fork in the road and took the left road. Soon she drew up in front of the castle, which looked imposing. There was no one around even though a few cars were parked in the car park outside the main archway. Maggie picked up her bag and walked along the stone path. Steps meandered off and a large tower rose up on one side. Bright red geraniums were dotted around in *Deruta* pottery urns and huge beautiful stone vases. She came to a heavy wooden doorway, which was open; it led to the laundry area where she met a large woman with a beaming smile who introduced herself as the housekeeper, Chiara. She led Maggie to where the family were gathered on the terrace.

Sitting under a pretty pergola covered in star jasmine was a young woman and two small children who chattered away in English as they coloured in sheets of paper with pencils. The young woman jumped up and made Maggie welcome.

'Hi. I'm so glad to meet you. I am Annie, and my children are Andy and Felicity.'

'Maggie,' Maggie introduced herself. 'I'm restoring the villa nearby.' She was invited to sit and offered a cold drink or coffee. The housekeeper hastened away and came back with a jug of homemade lemonade and two glasses. The children already had drinks and after initially being curious about their visitor, soon returned to playing with their art materials.

'I am so pleased to meet you. I heard there was an English woman who had bought the villa and was restoring it. Then I heard she had died but I didn't know any more than that.'

'That was my aunt. She had a sudden heart attack. I live in Australia so had to fly over at short notice and have been trying to carry on where she left off.'

Annie poured a glass of lemonade and sympathised with her, the children taking no notice of her as they focused back on their colouring books.

'How do you find the geometra, Antonio? Isn't he a dish?' Annie asked her.

Maggie took a deep breath.

'Well, he and I didn't hit it off at first and he didn't seem to think much of an Australian woman ordering him around. He is much better now as he seems to have got used to me.' Maggie replied, rather ducking the question.

Annie giggled. 'I love Italian men. They are so divine. Mind you I am not sure how faithful they would be. They enjoy looking at women too much!'

The two women sat and chatted but Maggie refused the offer of lunch. She still needed to get home and prepare for her visit to Fiesole. Annie kissed her goodbye on both cheeks, Italian style and saw her off from the front of the castle. The two children had come too to see what sort of car she drove. They seemed disappointed that it was only a small rental Fiat! Their father drove a fast sports car they told her. 'Very fast,' the boy said!

The weather was warm but the nights were still cool, so Maggie packed a long wool cardigan and sensible shoes, a couple of cotton dresses and a smarter dress and shoes for the evening.. She had her straw hat all ready and decided to use a lightweight backpack containing her camera and a small bottle of water as well as her wallet and small makeup bag. Having grown up in Australia, she carried a bottle of water everywhere, the habit so ingrained she never went out without it.

Chapter Seven

Next morning, Helen picked Maggie up in her car and they sped up the autostrada towards Florence (Firenze as noted on the signs). Maggie noticed the turn off for Incisa where The Mall was that Jonathan had told her about, and decided that one day, when she was driving herself, she would stop off there for some retail therapy ... if she had earned any money by then.

They stopped briefly on the autostrada for a coffee, the cafe busy but spotlessly clean. Helen, as usual, was very talkative but thankfully she didn't chat much while driving. Maggie found it interesting how Italians overtook quickly then swiftly returned to their own lane. The road surfaces were pretty dreadful with many potholes. Every so often they passed men trimming trees on the roadside, and Maggie saw large villas set amongst the hills as they drove. They passed the famous town of Cortona; another place Maggie vowed to visit. Cortona had become so busy since that American woman had written 'Under the Tuscan Sun' which was set there. She heard the author had to move house in the end.

As they drew closer to Florence the traffic grew thicker, and driving became tricky. Luckily Helen knew the way and they skirted around the city and up into the hills to the small, attractive town of Fiesole. Maggie noticed a smart hotel as they sped past. *Bet it has super views across the city*, she thought.

They drove into the car park of a small three-star hotel where the group was staying.

A very old town, Fiesole had an Etruscan/Roman amphitheatre, which Maggie was itching to visit. Thankfully staying just outside the town, everything was easily reached on foot. They checked in, handing in their passports, as required by law, and took the cranky old lift to their floor. It creaked and jerked its way up to the 2nd floor where they had adjoining rooms. They arranged to unpack and meet downstairs in about half an hour.

Maggie's room was cool, the shutters, as usual, closed; she opened them and strolled out onto a tiny Juliet balcony to gaze on the glorious view beyond. She could hardly believe how wonderful it felt to be standing here with so much history around her. The dome of the famous basilica in Florence glistened in the distance and hundreds of very old red roofs lay in front of her. It was as if a postcard had come alive.

Maggie quickly freshened up, then closed the shutters to keep out the sun, locked the door and headed downstairs. Helen was already below, a number of middle-aged people milling around her. Helen introduced her to the rest of the group, a mix of English and Americans, and one German couple. Another couple, younger men, Rick and James, had a tremendous sense of humour, and Maggie guessed she would enjoy their company. They lived near Pisa. The Americans were fun too but one English woman was so frightfully English, Maggie had to hide her smile. Then she was introduced to another English couple whose house was near Lake Trasimeno. The German couple were quite intense but friendly.

Seeing it was close to lunchtime they decided to wander into town to get a snack. One or two went their separate ways and Maggie found herself with Helen and the gay couple. They were very amusing and led them to a lovely café not far from the town square. They chose cool drinks and slices of focaccia with tomatoes and mozzarella and chatted to Maggie about their lives in Italy. They had all belonged to the group for many years and regaled her with stories of previous visits.

After lunch, Maggie decided to visit the Etruscan museum and the amphitheatre while the others wandered back to the hotel. The museum was fascinating and the black and gold Etruscan vases on display spellbinding. She shook her head as she studied them: that these stunning artefacts were older than the Roman era was hard to imagine.

Wandering back to the hotel, Maggie wondered about Jonathan – he'd texted her over a week ago to say thanks and that he was enjoying Florence, but where was he now? Just then she heard an email pinging in to her phone. Co-incidentally it was from Jonathan. Still on a high from Florence, he told her she must visit the basilica and the beautiful old pharmacy *Santa Maria Novella*. She would love it! He was now enjoying Portofino enormously. He'd met some people with a yacht moored there. *Typical Jonathan,* Maggie thought, *'He's bound to find some rich heiress to latch onto now*! she smiled.

As she put the mobile phone down voices turned her head. The two American women from South Carolina were approaching and she gave them a wave.

'Hi there, mind if we join you?'

'No, please do. Where have you been?' Maggie asked.

'Oh just pottering around the village. We have been before when we stayed in Florence. We love the area.' Their names, they reminded her, were Janice and Maisie.

'Well how are you enjoying it so far Maggie?' Janice asked

Americans always remembered names: they were very clever at it, Maggie noted. Unfortunately, when she was introduced to anyone, it went in one ear and out the other. *You really ought to buck up and copy the Yanks.*

'Oh I love it all,' she said. 'I can't believe I'm actually here where everything is so old. To walk amongst the stones in the old Roman amphitheatre and imagine men in Togas and Centurions sitting or walking on the same ground I'm on is quite astounding.'

'Hmm. We thought the same when we first came to Italy. Now we rather take it for granted,' Maisie said. The women now lived in Italy all year round and loved it

The trio enjoyed sitting in the shade, talking about the history of Italy which, while the Europeans took it for granted, Maggie was still enthralled.

'Those Etruscan vases are something that don't look out of place in this day and age, do they? Weren't they a wonderful civilisation? I don't know much about them, do you? I've read more about the Romans who came along afterwards. It always staggered me how the Romans had central heating and baths. They also had latrines and then everything slid backwards in England when they left. I visited England years ago and learnt a bit about the Romans then but I was too young to take much interest.'

'Yes, if you are really interested you must go to Herculaneum and Pompeii. They even had fast food places and a place where people had clothes washed and ironed!' Maisie was particularly enthusiastic about Italy.

Maggie thought she would never get to see it all and would never tire of its myriad of treasures.

Nearer 6 o'clock, the rest of the group started to arrive. The Germans said they'd been on a long walk and the English woman, Emily, had fallen asleep for most of the afternoon. Another English couple, who had driven from Liguria, joined the party and seemed very pleasant. So far Maggie noted there were no Italians amongst them. The waiter came out and asked for any other orders and Maggie requested her usual Campari and orange.

They chatted about life in Italy and various visits to other gardens; the *vendemmias*, the picking of the grapes. That sounded fun, even if hard work.

'There are always local *festas* in the villages, which are great fun. Italians love dressing up in medieval costumes,' Helen told her.

'Time to change for dinner I think.' Janice and Maisie stood up and made their way indoors. Helen and Maggie followed. There would just be time for a lovely cool shower before changing for dinner.

Later on in the dining room, they dined on stuffed mushrooms, grilled lamb and small roast potatoes with rosemary. An excellent Tirimasu followed this and Maggie decided she would learn how to make it. She'd heard of a local American woman in the Niccone Valley who gave cookery lessons. She breathed a deep sigh: *when the villa is rented out and I have a cash flow.* The thought was never far from her mind. She would need to visit the real estate office in town to check out house prices so she would be prepared if she had to sell.

Next morning after breakfast, Maggie picked up her backpack and made sure she had her camera. Walking downstairs she bumped into Rick and James who were keen to see the gardens they were about to visit, in particular the *Limonaria*, which was a place where potted lemon trees were stored in cold, frosty winters, as they wouldn't survive out of doors. Helen came rushing down the stairs worried she was late, and nodded to the trio.

'These gardens are very formal and very Italianate. The huge pots of lemons are moved indoors in the winter so you will see how they do that,' James told her. 'The Limonaria would be a beautiful conservatory type building I am sure. The one in the gardens in Florence is magnificent.'

Helen obviously knew the two men well and they chatted about various restaurants in Lucca and Pisa before piling into a small mini bus. Emily, the English woman, was puffing as she rushed to get on.

'Late as always,' James muttered as she clambered up the steps.

Maggie sat across the aisle from them. Behind her sat the two American women, then the rest of the English members. The Germans had bagged the front seats very quickly, before the rest of the group had assembled which raised a few eyebrows. The driver was a very friendly Italian, and the guide, Eric, stood in for the group's organiser who unfortunately had fallen ill and was unable to attend.

Tyres crunched on the hotel's gravel driveway as their driver, obviously believing he was a Le Mans racing driver, set forth. Eric, their English guide, spoke at first in Italian then, realising they were all English speaking, reverted to English. Maggie breathed with relief. It would have been a wasted journey until she learnt more Italian otherwise.

The journey wasn't very long and they soon turned into a splendid wrought iron gateway and swept towards a grand palazzo that stood in formal gardens of box hedging, topiary and water features. Beautiful stone statues graced the surrounds and everything was lush and green. Maggie's camera was active as soon as she emerged from the bus.

The group gathered and toured the gardens, their guide fully conversant with the property and the different statues. They reached the *limonaria* where the lemon trees would be wheeled in to wait out the winter. Built like a huge glasshouse or conservatory, it was stunning. They were then shown into an elegant orangery where coffee and refreshments were served before the visit ended.

On returning to the hotel, the group dispersed. They had one more night here before returning home. They gathered at the bar for aperitifs where Maggie heard more stories about previous visits the group had made, almost always to interesting gardens, often entertained by the sometimes titled owners. She laughed when Emily recalled the strange grottos in one garden, and had wondered what went on there in the evenings. *A bit reminiscent of the Marquis de Sade perhaps*, she wondered '*and orgies!*

Emily, obviously disgusted by what she imagined had gone on, debunked it all as rumour. 'A couple of centuries ago, grottos were all the rage and were often decorated, somewhat gaudily though, with seashells and other ornaments. Tastes change over the years but the Victorians would have loved it!'

By the end of the trip, Maggie felt she'd made some new friends, in particular James and Rick. She promised to visit them when she came up to Florence. Emily she could take in small doses, but she enjoyed the company of Janice and Maisie. Helen was fine but did tend to talk too much! Anyway it was good to be in a social atmosphere again; she'd spent far too much time on her own restoring the villa and garden.

As she sipped her customary Campari, her mobile phone zinged with a message – from Antonio! He wondered if she had arrived safely, and asked was she enjoying her visit. She nearly spilt her drink. Composing herself for a few moments, she texted him back saying how much she loved it, especially Fiesole and its history.

Well stone the crows! Fancy old Mr Arrogant bothering to check how I am?' And indeed she did still find him arrogant and stiff – so different from the men she knew in Sydney who were far more easy-going.

That evening they dined inside, a cool wind making it too uncomfortable to sit on the terrace. This time they were served veal escalopes, and a delicious gelato with almond biscuits for dessert. Maggie loved the intense flavours of Italian food, especially the fresh tomatoes. The only thing she disliked was the unsalted Umbrian bread. *Very unappetizing!*

Helen suggested they leave soon after breakfast so Maggie retired fairly early, though read her Donna Leon book about Venice for a while, realising she really ought to find a book featuring Florence, just to get the feel of the city. Books in English were hard to obtain and she tended to order them on-line. Helen recommended a superb bookshop in Florence, just near the *Duomo,.* which also had a café and an English section. This made a visit to Florence even more imperative.

They drove home, skirting Lake Trasimeno and, instead of driving through Tuoro and the Niccone Valley, they drove through Passignano, the place Maggie had first stopped on her way to the hotel.

'There are a couple of very good restaurants here with views over the lake. And over there, see the islands? You can visit those. There's a ferry from Passignano to the bigger island, Isola Maggiore … you can just see it in the distance, and then further around the lakeshore is a small village called San Feliciano where another ferry leaves for the small island of Polvese. This is a natural island with no cars and well worth visiting. The other island there is a little more commercialised … has more tourists because of the lace-making industry.'

Maggie hoped George wasn't quite as chatty as his wife but still looked forward to going to their house. She hadn't been to many local homes, apart from Francesca's, opposite the castello.

As they drove up the very twisty road into the hills, Helen concentrated more, became quieter, as every so often a crazy Italian driver would tear down the hill in the opposite direction, almost on two wheels.

They drove past a church in one village.

'There's a fancy hotel just around the corner from here. The Americans just love it.'

Just then the clock struck noon, and The Angelus echoed all across the hills – such a wonderful sound. And the scenery they drove through was glorious.

'You have to be careful driving along here at night. as *istrici* are a real menace,' Helen said.

'Istrici?'

'Porcupines. Their sharp quills can puncture a tyre in no time. And then there's the wild boar to contend with …

'Just over there,' she pointed across to the left, 'is a pretty hilltop village where the locals put on an opera every summer. It's well worth going to see. You get your tickets in the local *tabac* there. If you go, take a warm wrap. It gets very chilly up there at night even in summer. One year it rained during the opera and we all had to rush inside the church. The opera continued indoors where the acoustics were actually much better than in the open air.

'Luckily the local Catholic Priest was very much in favour of the opera so it was no problem. It's held later on in the summer, sometime in August. There is a lovely little restaurant in the village which overlooks the valley … definitely worth a try. A local family runs it and the mother helps with the cooking but the service is notoriously slow. If you go there, be warned: leave yourself plenty of time!'

They drove around the next bend and, lying in a slight dip, lay her village with the villa spread out before them. The castello stood broodingly looking over the valley: a stunning sight. Farmers were busy in the fields, using noisy old tractors to cut the crops. Maggie wondered if they were all relics from the last war as they looked and sounded so ancient. She noticed the patchwork fields had changed from brown to golden. There was always something to watch. She pointed out the villa to Helen and suggested she and her husband come up one day and see it.

'And you must come and visit us,' Helen reminded her. 'We're only a few kilometres further on from the town.'

'I am not sure exactly where Montone is?' Maggie noted.

'It's not far at all. Montone is fairly medieval, and very hilly, with steep cobbled streets but stunning views from the top. There are a couple of beautiful churches and a bar or two where you can have coffee or get a light meal. We have a film festival every year and had terrific excitement some years ago when Colin Firth was given the Freedom of the town. They showed "Pride and Prejudice" which the locals just loved. He spoke beautifully in Italian, as of course he is married to an Italian and is fluent in the language.'

Maggie wished she'd been there then too. Colin Firth was sexy and the vision of him rising from the lake in the BBC film of "Pride and Prejudice" was forefront in her mind.

When they reached the apartment, she invited Helen in and they whiled away the time eating sandwiches and drinking coffee until Helen had to leave for Perugia airport to pick up George that evening. His elderly mother had perked up during his visit but, as she was in her 90s, he could have to rush back there any time she had a problem.

Chapter Eight

Maggie settled on the sofa and put her feet up, wanting to finish her book about Venice and the incredible Police Inspector Commissario Brunetti. She loved the way what the family ate and their daily lives interweaved through the pages of the books Donna Leon wrote; it was almost as if she breathed and lived the lives of the Venetians when she read each chapter. As she lay reading, her phone rang. It was Antonio. *Heavens, this is becoming a habit!*

'Ciao Maggie, how was your trip?'

'Wonderful. I loved every minute of it. Is there something wrong?'

'No. Nothing at all. I just wondered if you would be free tomorrow evening to have a meal with me?'

Maggie nearly fell off the sofa. Disguising her surprise, she responded quite calmly: 'Yes, that would be fine. Where and when?'

'I thought I would take you out to *Calagrana* in the Niccone Valley. You might enjoy that. It might be too cold to eat on their terrace but you can see the views from there before we go inside. The food is very good.'

'Great. I would like that very much.'

'Shall I pick you up at 7.30? Are you going up to the villa during the day to see what's been happening while you were away?'

'Yes to both. That time is fine for me, and yes, I am going up to the villa. I want to see how Andreas is getting on trimming the long grass by the road and other jobs he promised to do for me. I also have to take the rental car back and pick up my new car.'

'That is great. However, I have to go to Perugia for a meeting so won't be around but I will see you at your apartment tomorrow evening. I do want you to see what you think about the bathroom at the cottage and see if it's what you wanted. I am pleased you have the car sorted out.'

Maggie put her phone down. *Wonders never cease.* Life was beginning to look up with all this sudden social activity! Then her mind wandered off. *What am I going to wear?*

Then her thoughts ran. What had caused Antonio to ask her out, given he was usually so standoffish? *God,* she prayed, *please don't let there be something dreadful happening at the villa and he is breaking it to me gently. But then I would see what is happening tomorrow.* Nevertheless, she couldn't concentrate on her book now – Commissario Brunetti would have to wait another day to solve the murder.

The next day she drove up to the villa and was delighted Andreas had trimmed and scythed the long grass. He now worked at the end of the garden but, as he had earmuffs on, he didn't hear her arrive, nor apparently did he hear the wretched, barking dogs in the neighbouring, possibly illegal, kennels. She hated seeing them restricted by long chains which was all that kept them in the yard. Sometimes she threw them some left over pieces of meat, which they devoured hungrily.

Walking down the garden, she noticed how clean and sparkling the pool looked. The plants were all doing well and were kept alive with a drip-feed irrigation system. A newly planted crepe myrtle tree that reminded her of Sydney was also doing well. She had forgotten its botanical name but thought it was something like Lagerstroemia. Anyway it was beautiful and the prostrate rosemary was beginning to hang down attractively from the top of the walls. The oleanders against a deep blue sky were riveting. What a difference from when she first arrived and the garden didn't exist. She hoped her aunt could see it from wherever she was, probably somewhere in a botanical heaven.

The cottage was open, the painters still finishing up. They smiled and said hello. Umberto, the boss, eagerly showed her the finished bathroom, and proudly held the door open. The tiling was superb. A deep bath ran along one wall and a large, glass-enclosed walk-in shower stood in the corner. She loved the feature tiling she'd chosen and thought it looked clean and fresh.

She waved goodbye to the workers and started to climb into her car when a horse came trotting up the hill. The huge shiny black beast reminded her of her childhood book 'Black Beauty.' The man riding it reined it to a halt before it reached her. He gazed at her for a moment then took off downhill towards the lake that belonged to the castello. It was almost like a scene from a movie.

As she drove towards the castello, Francesca came out waving to her. Maggie pulled in at the house.

'Ciao, do come in and have a drink with me,' she called.

Maggie locked the car and walked inside.

'I have news for you.'

'Oh I hope it's good news!'

'Yes, I have found a cleaner for you for the villa. Her name is Daniella and she lives in the village, near Andreas.'

'Oh, that's wonderful. I have to rent it out this summer. With all the work that's been done it needs to start paying for itself. I'm hoping a photographer can come soon and take photos for the website. I need to get it out there quickly.'

'Renting it out won't be a problem, I am sure. There are plenty of others around here, which rent easily and they are not as beautiful as yours. My partner knows someone who is a professional photographer and would do it reasonably for you, I am sure,' Francesca said.

Maggie sat down and they chatted, Francesca interested to hear about the trip to Fiesole.

'You really must go to Firenze. Also go to The Mall on the way. You will see so many beautiful fantastic designer shops. However, it is not cheap even so. There is another Mall, the '*Valdichiana*' Outlet Village, not so far away and its cheaper. Perhaps you would like to come with me as I am not so busy with work at this time of year. There is also a good café to have lunch so we can enjoy a day out there if you would like. Also I have asked my friend about you teaching English for Italian students and she will call you with the details.'

Maggie nodded keenly to both ideas. She needed to replenish her wardrobe and the thought of buying some Italian shoes was something she could get quite carried away with, and going with a local would be useful.

The rental car was returned to the office in town. Thankfully, she didn't have to drive it back to Perugia airport. Then she walked around the corner and picked up her little red Fiat … with the sunroof! It was the cutest little car she'd ever owned, and of course it needed a name. *Bambini*, seemed so apt for it.

Thinking about her dinner date later that evening, Maggie drove home and showered. She chose a simple black linen dress with a slight slit up the side, paired it with some pretty sandals, and finished it off with a row of tiny pearls around her neck. She also picked out a pashmina in bright pink, which might be useful if they lingered on the terrace.

She'd heard about this restaurant from other people and was keen to try it. She also wondered what it would be like going out with Antonio. He was quite an enigma and she had no idea if the young woman she had seen him with was his regular girlfriend. He had definitely softened up recently, but still appeared somewhat arrogant.

Antonio picked her up, looking quite handsome in a linen jacket and chinos. He wore a beautiful pair of Italian leather shoes.

Maggie sighed. She really needed to go shopping and buy herself some decent outfits. The last few months had been taken up with working on the villa and the garden, with no time for personal things.

'You look very elegant,' Antonio said, eyeing her appreciatively as he opened the car door.

He drove them out of town along a road that zig-zagged around the little village at the head of the Niccone Valley. They passed a beautiful church and drove along the country road, passing a vineyard and fields of sunflowers. There were fields full of tobacco plants, like many in the area. He seemed a careful but masterful driver and, like most Italians, drove fast.

They took a sharp left hand turn over a small bridge and wound their way up into the hills; a pig farm lay on one side and she could see cattle being shepherded into barns on the other. Antonio swept into the car park (*no Italian could drive slowly,* she thought!) and they stood looking at the view in the gathering twilight. She could see the road snaking through the valley with hills either side, or rows upon rows of sunflowers which bend their heads in whatever direction the sun was shining.

Antonio helped her out of the car, locked it and they climbed the steep steps towards the restaurant and soon reached the terrace. From the buzz of noise coming from inside it was obviously full of patrons. In the summer most people ate outside but it was too cool yet to do so.

Maggie noticed a sign for their guesthouse (*Agriturismo* in Italian*)*, and an announcement that cookery lessons were available. *Aha!* Maggie thought. *I have two choices of where I could learn cookery. Here, and the American woman's further back in the valley.*

Antonio held the door open for her and a friendly woman, obviously English, welcomed them. She greeted Antonio warmly and was introduced to Maggie. From the open kitchen window that looked into the restaurant the chef could be seen toiling in the heat. He noticed Antonio, waved and called, 'Ciao.' The owner's wife showed them to a table by the window.

'Ciao, good evening. Would you like the menu in Italian or in English?' she asked Maggie as she lit the table candle.

Maggie replied firmly, 'In Italian please.'

Antonio smiled.

They chose homemade pate with chilli jam followed by pork filet. Antonio asked what wine she would prefer and she chose a glass of a cool white wine from the Veneto area. Antonio had a *Multipulciano* red wine, only one glass he said as he was driving and it wasn't worth risking a drink driving conviction.

'Someone I know was caught over the limit, had his car confiscated and thought he would be clever and buy it back at the Police auction. Sadly, one of the officers liked the car and managed to buy it before the auction. It wasn't strictly legal but who was going to argue?'

Maggie smiled and nodded. 'I've read about Italian law courts and cases that have gone on for years, even when they got to Court. And what about that dreadful case in Perugia, the one where the young English girl was murdered. That American woman and her boyfriend stood trial, and then it was dismissed!' She shook her head. 'I don't have much faith in the Italian legal system at all.'

'You also have the case of Berlusconi, the ex-Prime Minister. That case is dragging on and on as well. Talking about Perugia,' he changed the subject, 'I spend quite a bit of time there on business. Have you been there yet?'

Maggie shook her head. 'I've hardly been anywhere yet, except the lake, Fiesole and Assisi.'

'Well you should go to Perugia. You could come with me when I am spending the day there and you can wander around and visit the sights. There is a small sightseeing, open-top bus tour you could do. It will show you the amazing Etruscan arch and all the wonderful things including the famous fountain in the main piazza. Where I park the car, we can go up on an escalator through the ancient parts which date from the Etruscans and then the Romans and you emerge in present day Perugia.'

'I'd love that. It's time I saw more places.'

Their food arrived and they savoured the meal Alberto had cooked – the delicious chilli jam, the pork filet – in portion sizes that allowed her to finish off with a lemon soufflé.

Maggie felt her stomach. 'I'd better not eat too many meals like this or I won't fit into my clothes,' she laughed.

During the meal, Maggie learnt more about Antonio's childhood and his English mother who was back in England at the moment as her parents were elderly and needed help. His father had taken time off from his own business and was visiting relations in Sardinia, this being a good time of year to visit. He had a brother working in Rome and another one in Florence, so at the moment Antonio was the only one living at home. His parents would be back in a few weeks.

At the end of the meal, Antonio bought a jar of chilli jam and gave it to her before they wandered outside and Maggie was glad of her warm wrap. It was indeed quite chilly and very dark. They followed the little lights on the edge of the steps that guided them to the car park. Maggie was surprised how much she had enjoyed the evening.

Antonio drove them back to town, the operatic CD he had put on lulling her into a sleepy, thoughtful mood – she almost had to pinch herself … to think she had actually been out to dinner with Antonio.

As they turned into the area outside her apartment, Maggie asked Antonio if he would like a nightcap.

'I had better get home as it's quite a way to go and I don't drink coffee after lunchtime.'

He pulled Maggie towards him and kissed her, passionately, and she thought it just as well he wasn't coming up with her. Her heart raced and it was all she could do to tear herself away. How different it felt from the cool relationship they'd had up to now. His dark eyes darkened with desire and he looked sorry that he had to rush off. Maggie fought to control her heart beat, and her rolling senses. He had put her in a turmoil.

'I will ring you about coming to Perugia.' Antonio said, handing her the jar of chilli jam. 'I have a couple of very busy days to get through first.'

His car roared off and Maggie felt a bit bereft as he left. *'Oh my goodness! Don't tell me I'm falling for an Italian, and especially Antonio! No, no, no!'* But memories of that kiss lingered. If he had come inside, Maggie knew she would not have been able to resist him.

The next day she received a call from somebody from the gardening group inviting her to lunch in a few days' time. It was somewhere not far from the lake and there would be quite a few of the group attending. Maggie asked if she could bring anything and the woman sounded surprised.

'No thanks, my dear. It's no trouble and I look forward to seeing you on Sunday.'

That's not like Australia, Maggie thought, *where everyone brings a plate. Maybe I should take a bottle of wine, maybe a white from the Veneto, or a red from the Montepulciano area. But I don't know what is a good one, so maybe chocolates instead. Maybe some Perugia chocolates, they're delicious.*

Thinking about the wine, she realised she hadn't been to the wine bar near the local gas station. It advertised simple meals and she decided to try it that evening. Another bar was further along the street, but it was rather noisy, and not her sort of place. The wine bar with its pretty pergola draped in flowering plants and outdoor tables and chairs suited her better. She was greeted warmly by the owner, a large jovial man, and his slender dark-haired wife. Their son, who also helped out, had such classical features he reminded her of a statue of a Greek or Roman God.

Maggie tried a few local wines, including *Sangiovese,* the grape grown near the lake, but she wasn't too keen on it. Then she tried a light rose wine, which she preferred, the staff helping her choose the different wines. For her meal she had a choice between veal or pasta and she noticed one or two other locals already enjoying a meal, the young son chatting to her as his mother prepared the meal. Her Italian had improved with the lessons she'd received, and she hoped by persevering she would eventually become fluent. With only a few tables, the bar was pleasant and intimate, and the family made her feel very welcome.

The next morning, Maggie drove up to the village of Montone to have a look around. It was as Helen told her: very steep with steps cut into the stone pathways to enable villagers to walk around the hilltop village, and the churches were beautiful. She found a bar and enjoyed a cappuccino while listening to the church bells resounding around the streets. A priest walked past and nodded to her, and she felt she could almost be living in the past as the priest in his vestments and the old buildings probably hadn't changed in centuries.

Just after noon she made her way to Helen's house on the outskirts of the village and enjoyed lunch with her and her husband, George. George was a quiet, studious man, a complete contrast to his wife. A couple of other cars were parked in the driveway and, clutching a bottle of wine, she walked to the door. Feeling confident with her choice of present, a rose recommended by the wine bar owner, Maggie rang the doorbell – it sounded like 'Westminster chimes', like the chiming of a clock her grandmother had owned.

George opened the door and introduced himself. 'Please excuse the doorbell, it always astounds visitors,' he said. 'It makes us think of home in England!'

Maggie smiled. She thought it would be fun to have 'Waltzing Matilda' for a doorbell, but then thought not. It would be rather crass!

The lunch party was held inside due to the wind. Maggie met two other couples she had met in Fiesole and the pleasant company made the time pass quickly. Helen served steak and mushroom pie and creamed potatoes, a pleasant change from Italian food. Although Maggie loved the local dishes, she wondered about ethnic food, as she hadn't seen any Chinese or Indian restaurants around.

'Are there any ethnic restaurants around?' she asked Helen.

'Not many, they're mainly in the cities like Florence. Many Italians think foreign food is something that comes from another village! I think there's a Chinese restaurant somewhere but that is all.'

Helen's and George's house was pretty but quite un-Italian, with chintz curtains and lots of ornaments, like they were living in another part of England. They had lived here for about 30 years and spoke Italian well. The other couple hadn't been here as long and one couple were nearer Maggie's age. They were based near Perugia where the husband worked in International Law. She enjoyed the afternoon and she found it interesting to hear more about the garden group.

'Do you think you will stay here in Italy or return to Australia once you have restored your place,' the lawyer asked.

'I really don't know but at the moment I am loving it here and don't feel homesick for Australia so far. It might be a different story in the winter as I'm not used to the cold.'

The couple said they were fortunate as they could fly back to the UK when they liked. Their only problem was that all their friends thought they could come and stay, which meant they were exhausted in the summer. They said they might have to pretend to be away a lot of the time. So many people thought they were on holiday too but both worked so it was very difficult.

'Guests are like fish: they go off after three days,' she said half-jokingly.

Maggie thought she would love to have some friends coming to stay but could see it might become a problem. Freeloaders were well known all over the world.

Maggie drove up to the villa the next day and the dogs barked furiously as she approached; she could see them straining on their awful chains as she passed. *That wouldn't happen in Sydney. The rangers would be after them for animal cruelty.*

Antonio's absence was noted – he had a meeting in Perugia. He also said he'd be in Perugia the following week and would take her with him. He'd sounded upbeat and friendly when he'd said it, and Maggie's stomach fluttered when she recalled his voice. She realised she actually looked forward to seeing him again.

The pool had been filled with water and sparkled in the sun and she was relieved there hadn't been a leak or other disaster. Now, at last, she could get the photographer and advertise the villa for summer lets.

As she left the villa she passed the dog kennels again. The owner's son was there kicking one of the dogs. Maggie stopped the car and chastised him severely in a mixture of Italian and English. Nevertheless he got the message and threatened her back with his fist.

Returning to the car, Maggie slammed the door and drove off, fuming. She remembered the warnings she had about that man but didn't care. She hated any sort of animal or child cruelty.

The real estate office was close to the wine bar so she popped in to enquire about the sale of the villa. *Just in case I run out of money,* she thought. The sales guy wasn't very hopeful as the market had really dropped in Italy. Also, a place that was neither finished nor fully furnished would be hard to sell. He gave her a ballpark figure anyway, which made her feel depressed. It really was imperative that she get the house on the website and fully booked for the season. She also enquired about rental prices, which seemed quite attractive.

That afternoon, Antonio rang to say he'd finished early and would she like to meet up? Maggie suggested he come to her apartment for a meal. She then rushed out to the butcher's as soon as siesta was over. She had made them laugh once when she'd asked for a butterflied leg of lamb, using the words she'd looked up in her dictionary. At first they were confused – it wasn't something they had ever heard of – then one of them quickly realised and they prepared it perfectly. She loved the local Italian sausages from there and realised she didn't know what sort of food Antonio liked.

Thinking back to what they'd eaten in the restaurant in the Niccone Valley, Antonio obviously ate meat so she bought two filet steaks. She nipped into the small *alimentari* next to the butcher and bought some cream. Thankfully she had some fresh vegetables and figs at home. She had a tub of marscapone in the fridge and knew he liked anchovies. She managed to get some olives stuffed with them. So strange they were called '*alici*' and she was quite pleased with herself for remembering the Italian word.

When Antonio rang her doorbell that evening, Maggie's heart flipped. She let him in and he hugged her tightly.

They enjoyed the meal – tender steaks with cream and brandy, green salad with rocket and baby spinach leaves with an olive oil and balsamic dressing, followed by fresh figs drizzled with honey and marscapone. Throughout the evening they chatted about their lives, their childhoods and how different they had been. Maggie put on a CD in the background, a lovely soft recording her friend in Australia had made. It was hauntingly beautiful with tones of Enya.

A slight tension in the air and Maggie knew that whatever happened tonight, she just wanted to be with Antonio. With her stomach a mass of butterflies, she could hardly finish her meal. They moved across to the sofa and Maggie was soon lost in Antonio's arms. He kissed her passionately and his sultry dark eyes darkened with desire. As he caressed her gently, she shed her T-shirt and he kissed her breasts. Maggie pulled him to his feet and led him into the bedroom and they made love before falling asleep.

In the morning, she woke first, to the birds singing in the large plane tree outside her window. Antonio hadn't stirred and she savoured his face in repose. She knew there was no going back; she was definitely falling in love with him. The last thing she thought she would do was fall in love with an Italian, especially this one.

'They simply have no staying power,' she'd always been told.

Moving into the bathroom, she showered and was in the kitchen making coffee when she heard Antonio up and about. He came into the kitchen, his hair still damp from the shower, and put his arms around her. She felt completely lost again and overwhelmed. What on earth had happened to the sensible Maggie of a few weeks ago? Her heart thudded and she lost her appetite again.

'Antonio, please tell me why were you so unfriendly towards me when I first met you?'

His eyes hooded a moment, as if he'd been expecting this. 'I thought you would be a brash young, spoilt Australian girl, someone who would want to maybe modernise the house in an unattractive way. I was prepared for that, but when I met you I found I was wrong. I am sorry. I was also annoyed with myself for finding you attractive too.'

'Oh. Well I thought you were very unpleasant and very arrogant,' Maggie replied.

Antonio kissed her then said, 'I have to go to the office for a meeting. I am sorry for what went on before. I was trying not to like you especially as I thought you would be returning to Australia.' He hugged her, held her tightly as if to convince her of his honesty.

Reluctantly, she waved him goodbye and he said he would ring her later. Maggie couldn't believe what had happened. *The last man I thought I would fall for,* she thought.

She sat with her head in her hands, her coffee untouched in front of her. This relationship was something she hadn't planned on. From his initial impression of her as a spoilt young woman, their relationship had suddenly changed, and the speed was unsettling. There was a definite physical attraction but Maggie had always thought of Italian men as Lotharios and not to be trusted. Then she remembered his girlfriend.

The mobile phone rang, startling her. It was Annie from the castello inviting her and a partner to a Masked Ball they were planning, the theme 'black and white' and if possible they were to wear masks. It sounded fantastic.

Maggie put the phone down and pondered where to buy a mask. She'd seen them for sale somewhere and hoped Antonio would be free to accompany her. The event was in about ten days' time. Their relationship was definitely moving forwards at quite a pace. Maggie felt powerless to stop it, as every day she didn't see Antonio, she felt bereft. No man had ever made her feel like this, and she wondered if it was nothing more than a holiday romance, certainly on his behalf. That was a thought she really had to quell.

It's time I spent some money shopping as I need something to wear.

She rang Francesca and asked if she would like to go shopping to the place she had mentioned before and, as Francesca and her boyfriend had also been invited to the ball, they arranged to go shopping the next day. Francesca happily offered to drive them as she knew the way.

Later that day, Antonio rang her and said how much he'd enjoyed last night and hoped she would see him again. His voice held a slightly hesitant tone and Maggie assured him she had been very happy with his company. Thrilled that he'd called, she asked him about the ball and mentioned she was going shopping with Francesca. Antonio knew Francesca well it seemed, as they had been to school together.

Relieved Antonio would accompany her to the ball, she put the phone down in a daze. What this man was doing to her psyche was incredible! She couldn't wait to see him again! What she couldn't understand is why he had changed his opinion of her from his obvious disapproval initially. Perhaps she would never know.

Chapter Nine

The next day she left her car at Francesca's and they drove up the hill and on towards the lake. Francesca, like all Italians, was a good but fast driver and they were soon on the *raccordo* going towards *Valdichiano*. It was very near the autostrada that led to both Florence and Rome and quite busy, but Francesca knew where to turn off. Maggie appreciated that she didn't have to find it herself as it was quite out of the way. They parked in the huge car park and walked through an enormous brick gateway.

The complex was huge but attractively designed, with seats and cafes and so many shops Maggie didn't know where to start. She wanted to find a pretty dress, and some shoes. Turning to take in all on offer, she noted wonderful menswear shops, and a smart luggage store; there were designer sports shops and ultramodern kitchen shops which Maggie loved browsing in – she thought Italian designs were the best, and adored the Alessi designs but found some of the photo frames and ornaments incredibly fussy. She noted a pretty little carousel for small children and gelato shops …

Francesca suggested they first have coffee and plan which shops to visit.

The two women browsed through various shops like excited teenagers and eventually found a beautiful long dress in very light cotton and silk material for the ball for Maggie. They then hit the shoe shops! After buying a few pairs of shoes each, they decided to stop for lunch – shopping was such hard work! Then Maggie suddenly remembered she needed a mask. Francesca thankfully knew just the right store for that and wanted one herself. Both stocked up on dresses, shoes and alluring Venetian masks, they made their way back to the village, tired but happy. Maggie drove home to the apartment, showered and made herself a toasted sandwich, too tired to do anything else … except hang the new dress in the bedroom, and stow her new shoes – a pair of elegant high heels, and two pairs of pumps, all in soft Italian leather – in the closet. She had also purchased an evening bag with a gold chain which she draped over the hanger along with the stiff, dramatic black and gold Venetian masks. The whole outfit looked exotic and enticing.

Antonio rang that evening. 'How did your shopping trip go?"

Maggie swooned over *Valdichiano* and the stores they had visited and told him what she had bought.

She almost sensed he was smiling. 'I often go there,' he added, 'I buy my suits in the menswear shop, and I like to get my shirts from *Boggi*. Did you try the gelato?' Again she sensed him smiling.

"Yes,' she said more seriously. 'We sat on a bench eating your delicious gelato and watching the children on the carousel.'

'Good for you. Now for some more serious business. I would like to meet with you at the villa tomorrow. Most of the work is finished and it is now a case of signing off on the projects. Then on Friday I will take you to Perugia.'

This trip Maggie had been looking forward to.

In Perugia, Antonio parked in a large, underground car park and they travelled up various escalators through the remains of Etruscan and then Roman buildings. It was amazingly deep and the main part of the town was high on the hill. They finally reached the top and walked out into the sunshine. As she gazed at the hills in the distance Antonio pointed out Assisi where she had been a few weeks earlier.

They didn't have time for coffee as Antonio had business to attend, so they arranged to meet for lunch near the famous ancient fountain. Maggie made her way to where the bus tour started, where a small open top bus waited. She climbed aboard, paying the guide once she was seated. The bus drove off with about a dozen passengers and they had an excellent commentary, in English. She could almost touch the walls of the old buildings as they drove along the narrow streets. They were shown the wonderful Etruscan arch, and the *Duomo*, and the beautiful old fountain in the main piazza.

When they had returned to the original bus stop, Maggie alighted and wandered along the main street, the *Corso Vannucci*, her face set in a permanent smile as she walked towards Antonio: she was seriously falling in love with this guy. He grinned at her as they sat down at the table, seeming very unlike the arrogant man she'd first met. They picked at their pizzas and she knew that all she wanted was to go back to her apartment and take him back to bed.

Antonio gazed at her, almost as if he was reading her mind.

His business finished in Perugia, they walked hand in hand back along the beautiful *Corso Vannucci* until they came to the escalators down to the car park. Maggie marvelled at the experience. To be heading down to what had been an ancient civilization was astounding. The stunning brickwork and huge archways led to passageways many metres underground. Antonio told her that next time they would use the driverless train from the football stadium.

As they drove away, he pointed out the university, and where the dead English girl had lived. Either her flat mates or someone unknown had murdered the poor young woman, he recounted, doubting they would ever know the truth. What stuck in his mind was the nonchalant way the flat mates had reported what they had done that evening and didn't seem devastated by her death.

'Would you like to eat in the local wine bar tonight?' Maggie asked him as they drew closer to home. 'I tried it recently and it's excellent.'

'Yes, that would be good and I won't have to cook for myself. I will be pleased when my mother comes home and does all the cooking!'

They enjoyed a simple meal but it wasn't long before they found themselves back at the apartment. Antonio stayed the night again and they found it hard to tear themselves apart when it was time for him to leave.

The evening of the ball was thankfully warm and Maggie dressed in the new, sleeveless, long white dress with black edging and low 'V' neckline. It swished as she walked in her new high-heeled black sandals, keeping to the 'Black and White' theme. In case it turned cold, she carried a warm black pashmina, and the stunning black and gold Venetian mask. She wondered how she would recognise anyone when they were all wearing masks.

Antonio drove to her apartment and decided to leave his car in the street outside and they had ordered a taxi to take them to and from the ball. She had just finished splashing herself with *Guerlain 'Shalimar'* perfume when the doorbell rang. Antonio was on time. That was not usually an Italian trait but she supposed it was the influence of his English mother!

When he walked in, she drew breath. He looked so handsome in his black tuxedo and bow tie. She kissed him and grabbed her iPad.

'Stand still. I'm going to get a photo!' she cried. Antonio smiled and the photo was terrific. Then he reciprocated and took one of her, the light shining off her hair and stunning outfit making it picture perfect. .

'You look beautiful, Maggie. I want to whisk you off to the bedroom.'

She shook her head. 'The taxi will be here soon, otherwise we could have a drink before we go,' Maggie offered instead.

'There is no need for that. We Italians rarely drink unless we are eating food. Not like you Australians!'

Maggie thought sadly that he was right. The image of drunken Aussies at home was all too clear. She hated to see drunks, which was something she never saw in Italy. She did ask Antonio why once and he said that Italians didn't like to lose face. She could see the logic in that. Appearances were everything, which was why they dressed so well. No sloppy T-shirts going out in the evening, they were always fashionably dressed and she couldn't imagine Antonio in a singlet. She loved to watch the *'passigato'* in the evenings when whole families including the grandparents would wander around the streets, dressed to the nines.

They waited outside for the taxi, which came almost immediately, and directed the driver to the castello in the village. On arrival, they wandered between flaming torches along the driveway and through the big archway down past the main tower. Boxes of geraniums along the way were subtly lit and a string quartet played in the distance. They walked down the stone steps past a big marquee that had been set up on a level area towards the swimming pool. Here tables were laid out with drinks and canapés served by white-gloved waiting staff. They each stood with a glass of Prosecco, looking over the infinity pool that glistened in front of them. The architects were very clever and had designed it as a pool rather than a swimming pool. Dark, almost black, wide stone steps from one end reached into it, blending it perfectly in the garden, although with its dark water, Maggie wondered if there were any snakes lurking inside. In Australia she had been happy to use a clear pool, so you could see if there was anything nasty in the water. However, in this case, a bright blue swimming pool there would have been so out of keeping. Antonio was very impressed. As a Geometra, similar to an architect, he agreed with Maggie that it looked perfect.

'I would love to see the restorations they have undertaken in the castello,' he added. The restoration had been the talk of the local area; the amount the young couple were doing was an enormous undertaking.

'I am sure they would love to show you around. Even I have seen only the terrace and the kitchen area. And tomorrow we've been invited to a lunch here down by the lake so we could perhaps see more then.' Maggie had forgotten to tell Antonio this in the heat of their passionate evening.

'That's news to me,' Antonio said.

'I'm sorry. It just slipped my mind to tell you. You can come, can't you?' Maggie asked worriedly.

'Yes, I can, but must be back later in the evening as my mother is due back from England and I have to tidy the house. I will be picking her up in Perugia on Monday morning. Then my father comes back too from Sardinia sometime next week. My mother will go mad if the house isn't as she left it!'

'Well if I can help let me know.'

'No, I don't want you to see it all messy. You will have to come and meet my parents soon when they are home and then you can see it!'

Maggie hesitated, hoping his parents would approve of his new girlfriend. She had never asked Antonio if he had a girlfriend and if she was Italian. They had just slipped into their relationship and hadn't talked about previous liaisons, at least she hoped it was a previous one.

'Do they know about me?' she asked Antonio. 'You have never told me if you have any other girlfriends either.'

'Well they know I have been working at the villa and I spoke about you, but they don't know any more than that.' Antonio grinned. 'Too much information and they would be asking too many questions!' He laughed.

Maggie, however, detected a slightly forced tone to his voice. There was obviously some slight tension there and she worried. Immediately sensing a problem, she thought she would leave it until another day to find out.

'I did have a girlfriend whom I have known since I was a small child. However, it wasn't serious,' Antonio told her. 'Her parents and mine are great friends,' he added.

Maggie felt suddenly cold. She had a strong intuition his parents would not be too pleased he was going out with someone from Australia. She sensed trouble ahead. Anyway she would enjoy this evening and stop thinking about problems.

They wandered around enjoying the night air, the Prosecco and the delicious canapés. The musicians changed to a jazz band and then dinner was announced. They walked up the stony path to the marquee. With the masks in place Maggie hadn't recognised anyone. She had no idea where Francesca was or even the host and hostess. She hadn't met Annie's husband either so was looking forward to that. Huge table-plans sat on easels by the door and they found their place further inside the marquee. Tall gas heaters were strategically placed around the area as the weather was still cool. Once seated, everyone removed their masks and placed them on the table in front of them. Maggie noted that Francesca sat not far away, close to the top table – Francesca waving to her enthusiastically – and also close by, Annie sat with a man, presumably her husband. Everything was in black and white. A professional photographer who'd been taking shots while they were in the gardens now came inside and started snapping shots as the food arrived. Maggie almost pinched herself

– here she was, sitting in a castle in Italy, at a ball. It was as if she was living in a dream. Antonio smiled at her, making her heart flip in a frightening way, and he quietly squeezed her hand.

The evening passed far too quickly and, after the meal, there was dancing. Maggie found the bathroom in the nearby castle, where the ladies were directed (men had the portaloos near the marquee). As she reapplied her lipstick, Francesca came in dressed in a slinky black outfit that made Maggie say 'Wow!' They both laughed.

'You look stunningly elegant tonight,' Francesca said truthfully. 'Antonio can't take his eyes off you! You haven't met my boyfriend Gino yet, have you? Come along and meet him now.'

'Oh good. I also want to find out about his friend, the photographer. I need to get the villa photographed as soon as possible.'

They strolled back into the marquee where the dance floor was erected. Immediately Antonio came up to reclaim her. Francesco beckoned her boyfriend to come over and they were all introduced. Gino was a builder with his own business and Antonio had met him before. They chatted for a while and he promised to get his photographer friend to ring Maggie. Then Antonio took Maggie off to dance.

'I have worked with Gino before,' he told Maggie. 'He is very good. However, he was not able to work on your project as he was working on a big job on the other side of Perugia.'

Right on midnight, as the big clock on the tower chimed, fireworks exploded. Everyone wandered outside to watch the display from the other side of the pool. Against the black velvet sky, whizzing Catherine wheels and zooming rockets joined the stars, erupted in loud booms and poured cascading lights of every colour down from the night sky. The sky was a kaleidoscope of colour for nearly fifteen minutes, and Maggie wondered what on earth it had cost. It also made her homesick for Sydney and their wonderful New Year firework display over Sydney Harbour Bridge. She swallowed thickly – it was the first time homesickness had hit her this hard. Antonio put his arm around her and kissed her lightly on the cheek. She felt so safe and happy in his arms but wondered again if this was just a light-hearted fling on his part. She still had that uneasy feeling about Italians, but now she also sensed the tension with his parents. She knew instinctively there would be problems there. Unfortunately Italians were very family-minded, and if they didn't approve of her, she couldn't see any future for them.

Soon it was time to leave, and their taxi was waiting on the driveway outside the castello. They piled in and, as there was no traffic on the road, they were home quickly. As they entered the apartment, Maggie flung off her pashmina and Antonio his jacket; they were soon in each other's arms and kissing passionately. Maggie brought out a couple of glasses of cold water from the kitchen, and they slipped out of their finery in haste – the water sat untouched until the morning. They slept soundly after making love, it was nearly 8 o'clock when they awoke.

'Fancy a coffee, Antonio?' Maggie murmured in his ear before she rose.

'Yes, but you must come back to bed with yours.' He smiled. 'It's too early to be up.'

Soon, Maggie was snuggled up in bed again, the coffees growing cold on the bedside tables.

They finally arose and showered just after eleven. Antonio made fresh coffee but they decided to forego breakfast as they were due back at the castello for lunch. Maggie wondered how on earth Annie and the staff would be able to do lunch up there after such an event the night before. She was obviously used to entertaining on a grand scale. It had certainly been a night to remember.

Retracing their steps of the night before, they parked outside the castello and walked down to the lakeside where people were gathering. It was a glittering scene. All along the lakeside, beanth umbrellas, tables were set out with bowls of fresh tomatoes with *bocconcini* dressed in olive oil, and thick syrupy aged balsamic decorated with basil leaves. Maggie could now tell the difference between ordinary balsamic and one that had been aged for at least 8 years. The staff brought out big bowls of pasta and there were cold meats and salads. A variety of delicious cheeses followed and bowls of strawberries with mascarpone. Amazingly, a cute little ice cream vendor's stall on wheels served everyone delicious gelato. The vendor looked as if he came from a comic opera with his straw hat perched on his head, and a saucy pink and white striped umbrella shading him from the sun. She took out her camera and took some quick photos.

Using her limited Italian, Maggie chatted to many neighbours who lived in the village but whom she hadn't met before. Antonio knew many people as he'd been to school with them. She looked across the lake and could just make out the villa on the opposite hill but her cottage was out of sight. The sound of dogs barking made her remember the poor animals chained up there. She still hadn't got around to doing anything about them but vowed she would. The photographer had arranged to come the following day and she hoped to get the website up and running this week. It was such a worry and she was scared she had missed the market.

'Antonio, we haven't discussed my moving to the cottage. I need to do that as soon as it's finished. I only took the apartment for a short term so I can move anytime.'

'I'm not sure I am too happy with you living there on your own,' he frowned with concern. 'It might be different if someone was in the villa or you had a dog to protect you.'

'Well it's a question of money. I'm running out fast.' Maggie sighed. 'I could do with a job, and am looking into teaching English.'

'That sounds like a good idea. But, talking about the cottage, I am serious – you might need to think about getting a dog. Anyway, I think we should get an alarm installed first, just in case. Otherwise, of course, I could move in!'

Maggie smiled. It was probably a bit too soon for that. After the setback she'd had with Jonathan, she wanted to move slowly in this relationship. Not only that, she had yet to hear about his parents and what they thought of their relationship. He'd been quite hesitant talking about that.

'Just in case of what? Surely there are no problems here,' Maggie subtly ignored his offer to move in.

'Well, with all these illegal immigrants swamping the place, things aren't like they used to be. There have been a few nasty incidents. When jobs are non-existent, unpleasant things tend to happen.'

They resolved to talk about it in the morning when she would go up to the villa and check if there was anything else to be done to either the big house or the cottage. Maggie was keen to move in and decorate the cottage. She'd found someone to make curtains and in places had installed plantation shutters. The downstairs windows all had iron bars, as had the villa, which, while quite decorative, were also a deterrent against burglars.

Lunch ended soon after 4 o'clock and, after Annie's husband Jeremy invited them to come over anytime to have a look around, they walked back to their car with Francesca and Gino, who only had to walk across the road. Maggie wasn't sure if Gino had moved in with her, as Francesca's parents owned the house. In Italy, she had been told that when the son or daughter of the house married the parents would usually create an apartment in the parental home. With live-in partners, she wasn't sure what was the case.

Chapter Ten

Antonio picked up his bag from the apartment and hurried home to tidy the house for his parents' return. He was reluctant to leave but thought it propitious to be at home when his parents returned.

Maggie said she would see him at the villa after he had picked up his mother from Perugia airport.

She still had not questioned him about previous relationships or if he still saw his Italian girlfriend; she presumed not but until they sat down and discussed where they were going, it was the elephant in the room. She remembered Francesca mentioning Antonio and his Italian girlfriend, a beautiful model who lived locally, but that was before their relationship became serious. At that time Maggie wasn't interested in him at all so had let it go over her head.

Antonio rang after he had picked his mother up from Perugia airport, checking to see if Maggie was going up to the villa. His father, he said, was returning home in the next few days. Maggie detected the tension in his voice.

She drove up the hill, setting the dogs to their usual barking as she approached. Antonio was wandering around the cottage, checking everything was ready for the alarm to be fitted. Even though he hugged her but she sensed something was wrong and her stomach flipped over. They sat on a low wall while Antonio rang the alarm company who were due to install a system later that morning. He distractedly ran his hand through his thick black hair and Maggie swallowed thickly. She knew the mannerism, and took

took a deep breath, needing to know what was wrong.

'Antonio, what is the matter?'

He sighed. 'I picked up my mother and was telling her about meeting you and that I was going out with you. She was quite shocked, as she knew I had had an Italian girlfriend locally and she thought that was serious. The fact you are Australian took her back a bit. Also the girl I was friendly with is the daughter of old family friends. We have known each other since we were children.'

'Well, she is English so I would think she would understand.' Maggie exclaimed.

'She hasn't met you yet, and I am sure she will be fine once she has got used to the idea. I think she is worried you might drag me off to Australia!'

'That is ridiculous, and besides I don't know anything about your Italian girlfriend. How long ago did you finish with her? You have never told me about her. Was it serious?'

'I broke it off with her after we got together. I just knew that she wasn't the right person for me. We had just drifted along for ages and once I got to know you, I didn't want her in my life except as a friend. We have known each other forever. Unfortunately she doesn't want to stay friends.'

'Was she upset?'

'Very. We had never talked about marriage but she had assumed we would just carry on and marriage would eventually be at the end of it. I had no idea she felt like that,' Antonio said ruefully. 'I guess I was being a bit lazy not doing anything about it. I let it drift on as I was quite happy having someone to go out with but never dreamt she was that serious.'

'Oh dear. Well, we have never discussed our relationship so perhaps now is the time to do that.'

Antonio hugged her tightly and, when he looked into her eyes, he saw tears welling up.

'I think I am falling in love with you. I just didn't expect to do so and it has taken me by surprise. I didn't realise my mother would be so upset at my breaking up with Livia. My father I can understand as he and Livia's father were partners in business until recently.'

A lump formed in Maggie's throat, realising that to go against his family would be very difficult for him. She returned his kisses passionately, her best friend's voice rolling in her head at their passion: *Go get a room!* The fact their relationship might be doomed made her even more frantic, and she could hardly tear herself apart from him. The sound of a vehicle approaching, however, made them draw apart.

The alarm company van trundled up the hill and they stood as it drew into the parking area. Antonio chatted to them about what needed to be done, and Maggie wished her Italian was good enough to be able to do this herself. It had improved enormously but she still had quite a way to go.

The dogs' barking resounded around the villa, adding to the noise the men were making. They remarked about them and Antonio translated that the owner was well known as a rather unpleasant guy and they replied they also knew he mistreated the dogs. Maggie thought it was about time she did something about them. While it was a tricky situation, she hated animal cruelty.

As she waved Antonio goodbye, he said he would call in when he'd finished for the day, and told her not to worry as he was serious about her and it was nobody else's business.

Furious about the dogs, Maggie drove too fast down the hill — she overtook the postmistress in her little Fiat, who usually drove faster than anyone else, and nearly clipped one of the bends. Only then did she slow down. Anxious to talk to one of the women who ran the dog stall about the dog problem, she did so as soon as she arrived back at the apartment. The woman suggested they go and see the local veterinarian after siesta. Maggie agreed and said she would meet her there.

At the vet's, Maggie explained the dog problem, the other woman translating in Italian. There wasn't a lot they could do but they offered to inspect the premises as it was probably running illegally as a dog kennel business. With any luck he wasn't paying tax or something of the like, so a word in the right direction might sort out the problem. *A bit like Al Capone and how his tax problems brought him down*, Maggie hoped.

She returned to the apartment, gave notice of her intention to move, and arranged for a small local removalist to move her items of furniture the following week. There were lots of bureaucratic things to sort out and anything in that vein took forever in Italy.

As she sat at her laptop, she decided to contact one of the big rental companies about letting the villa next summer and also find a tenant for the winter. One had been recommended by some of the Garden Group, and she found the site quite easily and placed an advertisement for both. Having already looked up prices on other sites, she had an approximation of what to charge, and posted some beautiful photos the photographer had taken and sent her.

Just then her phone rang – her friends in Australia were hoping to come and stay with her as they were currently touring Paris. Thankfully it wasn't for a couple of weeks so they could easily be accommodated in the cottage.

The doorbell rang. Antonio stood on the doorstep with a beautiful bunch of flowers in his hand.

'I thought you looked a bit sad when I saw you so I brought you these,' he said.

'Oh, they are heavenly.'

He put them down on the kitchen benchtop and they were soon enveloped in each other's arms.

'Do you have to go home for a meal tonight?'

'Yes, my mother is expecting me. She also wants to meet you so asked me to see if you were free at the weekend to come to lunch?'

'Yes, that would be lovely.' Privately Maggie's heart sank. Not something she would look forward to.

'I will ask her which day she wants you to come but I also thought we should go out to one of the islands for lunch, just the two of us.'

'Oh, that would be heaven too. I have wanted to go to the islands for ages.'

'Well, there are two islands, one is quieter than the other but both are fine for lunch. The bigger one has a lace museum and you can buy lace there too. Just decide which one you would like to visit. We can always do the other island another time.'

What a choice, Maggie thought. The idea of lace making appealed to her, and that made her decision.

'Right, either Saturday or Sunday. I will ask my mother first, then we can go on the other day to Isole Maggiore. We will park in Passignano and catch the ferry over. I have a favourite restaurant there, which you will love. It is right by the lake and we can walk around the island first – there are about three beautiful medieval churches to visit that date from the 12th century. St.Francis landed on the island in 1211. When you have had your fill we will have lunch at L'Oso. If it's a nice day we can sit outside in the fresh air. Be warned, you would need flat shoes.'

Antonio kissed her and she waved him goodbye then put the

glorious blooms in a vase. *How Italian of him!* She was however very apprehensive about meeting his mother and father at the weekend. The fact his mother was English would surely be a plus point, and not being Italian wouldn't matter as much as it would in an all Italian family. She knew she was kidding herself as obviously his parents had looked forward to the blending of two families, and the fact that this ex-girlfriend was so attractive didn't help. Maggie sank into a chair: she wished she had taken more notice of her when she had briefly seen them on the street in the town.

She tried to push her thoughts elsewhere; tried to focus on the island visit Antonio was taking her to, but she tossed and turned all night, worrying about their relationship. She hadn't expected to fall in love and the fact that his mother was so hesitant about her being Australian worried her. What his father would think was another matter and she guessed it would be a huge hurdle to overcome.

Chapter Eleven

Next day Antonio rang to say his mother would meet her on Sunday, which left them free to go to the island on Saturday. While Antonio was busy catching up on projects Maggie drove up to the villa and met the alarm people who had just finished installing the system. They explained how it operated as best as they could with her halting Italian. Walking down to the villa, Maggie could hear Andreas using the weed-eater in the distance. She decided to check the oleanders at the bottom of the garden and sauntered along the fence line. As she reached the end wall, she noticed a pool of red pooling on the ground – it looked like blood. Hesitantly, she looked up … and screamed, and screamed. Impaled on the wall was a pig's head, gruesome in its death, and she reeled and ran; rushed back along the fence to where Andreas worked, oblivious in his earmuffs to her cries. She gesticulated wildly.

'Andreas, come. You must come. This is awful!' she managed to say in broken Italian. Andreas quickly understood it was serious and followed her along the path. He suspected she'd seen a snake but when he saw the pig's head he crossed himself and swore in Italian. It was disgusting. He told Maggie to take a photo of it with her iPhone, then he would get rid of it. This she did, then she rang Antonio. He immediately guessed it was retaliation because she'd complained about the dogs. He knew the people in the house were skating round the edge of the law and told her to be very careful. He would ring the *carabinieri* anyway, and was thankful he had arranged for an alarm system in the cottage.

Antonio rang back to say the *carabinieri* would look into it. They would send a patrol car up to the village and check out the situation. Maggie didn't have much faith in them as although they looked super elegant in their dark uniforms with the red stripes down the trouser legs, she felt they were pretty ineffectual.

She returned to the cottage and looked around, trying to put the sight of the pig's head out of her mind. The cottage looked cosy and attractive. She had arranged a delivery of logs for the wood-burning stove and found them stacked up beside the cottage. To keep busy she put on a pair of gardening gloves and moved a load inside to the log basket by the stove. She had stored some rugs in the villa, which she now fetched and put one on the living room floor and another in her bedroom.

Once she'd finished doing all that, she locked up and said goodbye to Andreas, and told him the *carabinieri* were checking up about the pig's head. Thankfully Andreas had deposited it in his little ape three-wheeler and covered it with sacking. If anyone wanted to see it, they could as he was going to take it back to the farm.

Calling in at the apartment straight after work, Antonio gathered Maggie in his arms and kissed her. 'I am very worried now,' he said. 'This pig's head is typical of the mafia; it is an ancient warning. While I am sure your neighbours do not know where you live in town, you might be in danger once you move up to the cottage. I do not wish you to move there now.'

Maggie shook her head. 'I will not be put off by them or their stinking attitude, Antonio. Obviously the vet has been there and perhaps something will now be done about the poor animals.'

He shook his head. 'Then we will have to make sure you are safe.'

Shrugging off this awful episode, they made plans for their trip to the island, and checked the Saturday weather forecast – it was going to be fine. Antonio booked a table at the restaurant, requesting outside if the weather was still good. The trip was something to look forward to and took Maggie's mind off the unpleasant pig's head fiasco for a time. However, it would haunt her for weeks to come, especially at night. Then they discussed her getting a job to aid the finances until a regular period of rentals was established. Antonio had spoken to a friend who agreed Maggie could run a short course teaching English to Italian students. She breathed with relief. That was also what Francesca's friend had proposed.

Saturday dawned sunny, with a light breeze and beautiful blue sky. At this glorious time of year the air felt so clean and pure. Later on, in the summer, it would get very hot and not so pleasant for sightseeing. Antonio called for her in his car and they drove up the road past the village and through the beautiful village of *Castel Rigone* with its lovely church; they stopped for a coffee and then took the winding road down to Passignano. The lake sat shimmering in the distance and Maggie could see a ferry plying back and forth to the island. They parked in the car park and walked hand in hand to the ferry terminal on the pier. Maggie looked over the boardwalk, and watched eels swimming around the rocks at the bottom of the lake as Antonio bought their tickets. The ferry approached and, when passengers disembarked, they walked on board and climbed the stairs to the top deck. Maggie was glad of a cardigan, as it was quite windy. The ferry left on time and she looked back towards the pretty village of Passignano. She noticed the ruined castle on the top of the hill, which she had seen on her first visit to the town.

The ferry stopped in Tuoro and Antonio pointed out where Hannibal had the famous battle in 217 BC when he defeated the Romans. According to folklore, he said, the lake had filled with blood and one of the villages was called *Ossaia* and the other *Sanguineto* meaning where they found bones and blood. They were very sad reminders of the battle when Hannibal's soldiers either killed or forced the Romans into the lake to drown. Maggie remembered her guidebook. She'd been too busy to read up about the island in it and decided to do so on her return.

As they approached the island, Maggie could see a church on top of the hill, and rows of yellow sun umbrellas at the water's edge which was the restaurant *L'Oso*. They had time to wander right around the island before lunch, and walked along the boardwalk from the ferry, past a café on one side and a souvenir shop which sold postcards and T-shirts at the end. She noticed the lace museum and a few old ladies sitting making lace on hard chairs outside, one old lady so tiny she could have only been about four feet tall. Maggie bought some lace handkerchiefs and tucked them in her backpack. They walked around the lower end of the island to the ancient wooden statue of St. Francis then up to the church on the hill. Inside, the frescos were stunning and she didn't begrudge the small donation requested.

'All the buildings on this island are very old,' Antonio said, 'and until the 1950s there was a huge problem with malaria caused by the mosquitos.'

'How many people live on the island?' Maggie asked.

'Probably no more than 35 or 40,' he replied.

He obviously knew the island's history and said he visited here because he enjoyed its peacefulness. Before long they reached the restaurant and were greeted by Sergio, the maitre'd, who knew Antonio well. He showed them to a lakeside table and explained the specials of the day.

They chose a small carafe of local wine and lake fish served with brightly coloured roasted vegetables sprinkled with fresh *parmesan* cheese. After a coffee and a glass of *limoncello*, it was time to walk to the ferry for, if they missed it, it was a long wait for the next one.

Antonio put his arm around Maggie as they passed a small shop selling gelato. 'That is Sergio's mother's shop,' he told her as they boarded the ferry.

'The other island of Polvese I will point out on our return trip. We will go there one day but to get there we have to go to a small place called *San Feliciano*. We will go early as there is a very interesting fishing museum I want you to see.'

Sitting inside the ferry as it was getting cooler, Antonio showed her *Polvese* in the distance and one or two other places of interest around the lake.

When he dropped her off at her apartment, he hugged her warmly and suggested she drive to his house about 11 am. She smiled and thanked him, and he roared off, her nerves immediately rising again about meeting his parents.

Tomorrow is going to be a very difficult day. Now think about what you are going to wear that will make a good impression.

After making a cup of tea she sorted through her wardrobe. She selected a lovely dress, which she would wear with flat shoes so it wouldn't be too over the top. The lace hankies she had bought on the island were a gift for Antonio's mother and she had already bought her some flowers. Then Francesca had told her Italian women rarely bought flowers for their homes, choosing to put them on their relatives' graves instead of those rather nasty plastic flowers that decorated those funny little houses that Emily, the English woman from Montone, had told her were tombs for the dead. Antonio's mother, being English though, might be more like Australians who loved fresh flowers in their homes. She had no idea what Antonio's father was like, but tomorrow all would be revealed..

Chapter Twelve

It drizzled on Sunday as she drove up through the hills, and Maggie considered them lucky to have had fine weather the day before. She drove slowly on the slippery roads, and wondered as she passed the castello if the family were still in residence. Antonio was still interested in seeing the restorations so she would try and find out when they would be there. Francesca's house had its shutters across the windows and there was no sign of life there. The church bells were ringing as she approached the beautiful church in Castel Rigone and many cars parked nearby. One day she would go there and enjoy Mass being said in Italian. It would be the nearest thing to a Latin mass, which she had loved as a child. Her convent school days were a happy but distant memory now.

Following Antonio's instructions, she turned off the road at a T-junction and followed it to a hilltop village she had not yet visited. People were spilling out of church and wandering across the road to the small café. Family lunches on Sundays were a favourite past-time in Italy and always included grandparents and extended family members.

The road twisted and turned down the hill, then she saw the sign for Antonio's parents' house – *La casa delle Rose* (the House of Roses). It had aptly been named: roses cascaded all over the garden walls and climbing roses were trained over the front of the house. It was a very attractive looking house with a shady portico to park the car and keep out of the rain.

As she drove in, Antonio hurried out to greet her. He opened her car door and hugged her.

'It's a shame about the weather. As you probably noticed, Italians hate going out in the rain and the only people around would be those going to or from church. It doesn't rain often in the summer and we will be glad of it in a month or two's time!'

Maggie smiled. She'd realised on the few rainy days that had occurred, people scurried around to stay out of it, and there was no *passeggiata*, or evening stroll.

She climbed from the car and hoped her nervy stomach would settle as she still worried over how Antonio's parents would take to her. They certainly hadn't sounded enthused, and she suspected his father would be furious that Antonio had finished with his friend's daughter. The light was missing in Antonio's expression and she feared they may have already quarreled over their relationship.

Maggie gathered up the pretty little gift-wrapped lace hankies and the bouquet of flowers and followed Antonio into the house. It was important in Italy to wrap presents beautifully as presentation and appearance was everything.

The house had cream floor tiles, and lovely high ceilings. She noticed a wide sweeping staircase going up to the second floor and a large archway to her right led to a formal living room. A door opened at the end of the corridor and a tall, elegant woman appeared, and introduced herself to Maggie as Eleanor. She was delighted with the flowers and took the small gift to open in the kitchen. She and Antonio followed, Maggie noting the white cabinets, the range cooker (similar to the one she had chosen), and the delicious smell of lunch cooking. A grey-haired man rose from a winged chair near a wood-burning stove in the corner.

'Welcome to our home,' Antonio's father greeted her, his English flavoured with an attractive Italian accent. 'I am Paulo.'

What a dishy man for an older guy, Maggie thought. A tall man, greying at the temples, he reminded her of Marcel Marciano, the film star, and she could see where Antonio's good looks came from. Then she noticed Paulo's scrutiny and was so pleased she'd worn a pretty dress and hoped she made a good impression.

Following Antonio into a room resembling a family room back in Australia, he took her raincoat from her and put it in the hallway on an old oak settle. Obviously Eleanor had brought some lovely old antiques from her homeland. Still feeling nervous, Maggie hoped it didn't show. Antonio sat down next to her and smiled at her reassuringly; she sensed he knew how she felt and gave him a rueful smile.

When Antonio's mother asked if she would like a drink before lunch she asked for a glass of water. As she sipped it, she scanned the house, which was decorated beautifully with an English influence. Eleanor busily arranged the flowers Maggie had brought into a straight modern vase, similar to one she had back in Sydney while Antonio answered his father's questions about a building project. She caught the furtive glances from Paulo and imagined him comparing her to the beautiful daughter of his closest friends.

Then he rose and went to the fridge; brought out a bottle of white wine.

'What would you like with lunch, Maggie'" he asked.

She noted it was a white wine, and simply nodded.

'I will have Montepulciano,' Antonio said.

'Lunch will be ready *subito*,' Eleanor said, mixing English with Italian. 'I checked with Antonio if you had any allergies or were vegetarian or anything like that,' she told Maggie. 'I once had someone for lunch who I didn't know was vegetarian, and I had made lasagne! It was a difficult thing to fix at the time and I just wish this person had thought to tell me in advance!'

'What on earth did you do then?' Maggie asked, empathic to her dilemma.

'Thankfully I had made roasted vegetables for an evening meal and they were in the fridge, so I warmed them up in the microwave and served them with crusty bread!'

Maggie laughed.

'That was so clever of you. I remember having friends to drinks and one was gluten-free and I had no idea. Thankfully the rice crackers I had with dips were alright for her but it is a bit of a minefield these days.'

Eleanor turned to Paulo and said something in Italian. Obviously they used both languages in this household. She could understand so much more now she had been living in Italy a few months.

They moved to the big chestnut table that Maggie had been quietly admiring. It had beautiful harp-shaped wrought iron at each end. The dining room chairs were upholstered, which was unusual – chairs she'd seen in other houses had been hard-backed, and the ones she'd bought for the villa were hard-backed with raffia seats. She hadn't seen any other option in the huge warehouse where she'd bought them.

'I love your chairs,' she told Eleanor 'I haven't seen any like this in Umbria, only very hard chairs!'

'Ah, I brought these over from England, as well as the sofas. I like comfort and when we were decorating our home years ago, there was not much choice. Italians didn't 'do' comfort in the old days.'

Eleanor asked how long she would be staying in Umbria, then Paulo asked Antonio quietly if he had seen Livia recently. Maggie wasn't supposed to hear as his mother showed her a book of Italian gardens. But her attention pricked up. This was the first time she had heard Antonio's ex-girlfriend's name. Antonio shook his head and said he hadn't. Paulo went on to say that he had seen her father in the hardware store in town one day but it appeared there had been a rift because of the broken romance.

Maggie, assuming Livia was the beautiful daughter of family friends, felt sad. She had caused this problem, and that didn't bode well with Antonio and her relationship. In the uncomfortable silence, she was sure they'd all thought the relationship would lead to marriage and unite two families. The conversation then turned to her restoration of the villa and again to when she would be returning to Australia.

'I don't know if I'm going back to Sydney. I'm enjoying living here and love the villa so I am moving into the small cottage next to it next week. Hopefully I can rent the villa out all through the season, as the restoration work has been very expensive and I'm worried that if I can't get enough bookings, I will have to sell it.'

Antonio's parents glanced at each other.

Then Eleanor asked her how she was going to fill in her time without a job and also how her Italian coming along. They chatted about her idea of renting out the villa later on in the winter as well as summer lets. And she mentioned her idea of teaching English to Italian students.

'I also thought I would take further studies at the University of *Stranieri* in Perugia,' she told them. 'Maybe you would like to come sometime and see what we have done with the villa.'

Antonio's father looked pleased. As a builder, he wanted to see what his son had achieved. Eleanor was also interested. She loved interior design and had wanted to be a designer when she was young. Unfortunately her parents wouldn't let her go to art school and she learnt floristry instead. She felt the atmosphere had thawed slightly but still felt on tenterhooks.

Antonio suggested they walk in the garden as the weather had brightened somewhat so they wandered out the back door. This led to a covered terrace with huge terracotta pots, probably from Deruta whose retail outlets were not far away. Maggie loved the look of these pots and vowed to get some for the villa and cottage, when she could afford it. The garden was terraced and full of flowering plants. A few houses dotted around the hills in the distance. After the rain, birds twittered in the trees, making this place beautiful and peaceful.

'Antonio, you haven't told me much about your previous girlfriend. You need to tell me what happened there. Your parents were obviously fond of her.'

He sighed. Obviously he didn't want to talk about it but shrugged before saying: 'As I mentioned before, she is the daughter of a great friend of my father's. We knew each other since we were very small. We just sort of drifted together a lot of the time and I guess she thought it was more serious than I did. There was certainly no intention on my part for anything else. However, when I first met you, I couldn't keep seeing her. She was very upset when I broke up with her and I thought we could remain friends. Unfortunately she was very bitter and that has rather spoilt the relationship my parents had with hers.

'She is very beautiful but I found sometimes I was getting bored with her as she was overly concerned with her looks. She is a model so I understand …'

'Oh dear, no wonder your parents weren't too keen on meeting me and asking when I was going back to Australia. It must be awful for them to have their friendship with her parents affected.'

'Oh well,' he sighed again, 'they will get over it. They thought you were just here for the summer and would be going home. Anyway, they will come around. You obviously got on well with my mother.'

Maggie reflected on the lunch. She had found Eleanor friendly but wasn't so sure about Paulo. She would have to win him over. In different circumstances, Eleanor and she would have lots in common, but of course she would stand by her husband.

They returned to the house and Maggie said she had to get back to her computer and finish building a website for the villa. Then the following week she would move into the cottage.

The journey back seemed much quicker and she felt a little tearful that Antonio's parents weren't overly impressed he had an Australian girlfriend. They had been polite and friendly but no more so than with anyone else they had invited for lunch

The next week passed in a blur. The website was launched at last and Maggie was delighted with the result. The photographs showed off the villa beautifully. Then came the day of the move. She bid her lovely old neighbour goodbye and gave her a box of Perugia chocolates as a farewell gift.

The removalist loaded her few possessions in quick time and she followed the van up the hill to the village. Francesca was gardening in their front garden as she passed and they waved to each other.

They arrived at the cottage and Maggie opened the door and turned off the alarm. She showed the men where to put the furniture and they propped the few paintings against a wall.

Maggie unloaded a bag of foodstuffs and, as the fridge had been turned on, put milk and other perishables away. She made the men moka coffee, which soon bubbled on the stove and filled the kitchen with a wonderful aroma.

The weather was beautiful so she and the removal guys had their coffee under the pergola; she paid them and they set off cheerily down the hill. She was now on her own. She checked her mobile phone for messages and found one from the Garden Group: they were organising a visit to a beautiful garden near *Pienza* called *La Foce*. She'd heard of this place and was keen to go. Iris Origo, the late owner and her husband (who was titled) had developed the land around the house. It had been in poor shape before the war and the Count had transformed it. When the war came, Iris arranged for a large number of children from war damaged areas to come and live in the house where she created a school and small hospital. Many of the *contradini* (peasants) also hid in the cellars during air raids. She'd heard how amazing all these people had been, hiding allied servicemen who'd escaped and were trying to get to Spain or somewhere else.

Antonio rang to see how she had fared with the move. He was in Perugia on business and would be home late. He promised to visit her the following day. Maggie hoped that was the real reason for his absence, and not because he worried over his parent's lukewarm attitude. She knew it would take some time before they would accept her, if ever.

Before switching off her computer, she checked her emails. Numerous requests had come in regarding renting the villa. Thrilled, she answered them immediately. Not wanting to miss a single booking, she brought out her diary and began blocking off dates. With that big problem out of the way, she turned her attention to her other big problem – relationship with Antonio – and wiped a tear from her eye.

Looking at her calendar, she realised how much she had to do before she could hold her 'opening' party; this galvanised her back into action for she had to get the cottage properly sorted out. She emailed out the invitations and left a message for Geoffrey on his mobile phone. He had returned to his house somewhere the other side of Perugia and said he was able to attend.

The cream and blue sofas looked inviting and Maggie was pleased with the blue cushions she'd bought to go on them. The new glass-topped wrought iron tables the blacksmith had made to go either side looked elegant, and he had also made the glass-topped dining room table. That would probably drive her mad as it marked so easily but lightened up the room. Thankfully she'd persuaded the painters to lime wash the dark beams, in the French style, rather than leave them. The old tiled floors had huge rugs scattered around, looking far more expensive than they really were. The table lamps, which she'd purchased in Gran Casa, were beautiful, and she'd never seen such wonderful designs in Australia as the huge selection she had to choose from here. Her bedroom was barely furnished; a fitted wardrobe, her *matrominiale* bed, which Italians called a queen-size bed, and two bedside cabinets made from chestnut wood. One day a couple of weeks ago Francesca had taken her to a furniture emporium on the other side of Citta di Castello and she had found them there, and a beautifully painted cream dresser with a floral motif. The cottage certainly had character.

Chapter Thirteen

Maggie emailed Antonio and asked him to invite his parents up one day to see the villa. Italians didn't drink much so the food would be the important thing. She knew she would need help in that department and wondered if Francesca could recommend someone.

As the cottage was tiny, she decided to hold the party in the villa, and was thankful the new cleaner Francesca had put her onto was due to start today.

'Ciao,' she greeted Daniella when she arrived. 'I wondered if you spoke any English?'

Daniella replied she only knew a few words, but what made Maggie smile was when she said she would do a 'deep clean' to start with. That certainly sounded promising. Danielle set to and with a few words of Italian intermingled with English as well as some sign language; the girl did a very good job.

Looking around the cottage garden afterwards, Maggie began planning what to plant. *Gaura* she had found out loved the heat and was very easy to grow and had a loosely spreading habit and was pretty; Lavender too of course and herbs, but many of those would have to wait till autumn. In fact she decided to wait till after her visit to La Foce to see what ideas she could gather from there.

There had been a few problems with her new dishwasher so she telephoned the repair company. It was such an odd name, translating as a dishwashing stove (*lavastoviglie*)! The phone message asked her to choose between five options, all in very fast Italian. Maggie listened to the message three times before she understood which button to press! She managed to make herself understood and the repairman booked her in for the morning.

Just as she was settling down to do her Internet banking, Antonio rang. His parents were keen to see the restoration work and wondered if tomorrow late afternoon be suitable. He said he would meet them in town and they could follow him up as they were going to a function for lunch. He hesitated and Maggie caught the change in his voice.

'Well, are you going to tell me what else is on your mind?' she prodded.

'Just that they, and in particular my father, are not happy I have given up my girlfriend.'

'Are they very angry about it or just disappointed?'

'Well my mother is the latter but my father is furious with me,' he replied sadly.

Maggie steeled herself. This could be the end of their relationship. Surely he would do what his father wanted. She shivered.

Turning her thoughts to their visit, she asked what she should offer them. 'Do you think they would prefer coffee or tea or maybe a glass of Prosecco?'

'Well just wait and see and please don't get worried about their visit,' he replied.

It was all very well for him to say that but she felt at a distinct disadvantage with his parents, especially being Australian. Also Italians often ceased drinking coffee after lunch, especially milky coffees. Maggie didn't want to make a faux pas on their first visit. She was glad the cleaning girl was coming in the morning and prayed the dishwasher should be fixed by then. It was Market Day so fresh flowers would be readily available and she thankfully had some of Alberto's wonderful pastries in the freezer. She would open up all the shutters so Daniella could dust them and the rooms would be open to the light when they came up. The only problem were the scorpions, which hid behind dark corners and she knew they might be disturbed. Thankfully Daniella would probably be adept at sorting them out but Maggie hated them.

Wednesday's skies were clear and blue, and she set off to the market early. She parked in the small square, which led to the main piazza. The usual gaggle of ex-pats clustered around the bar in the corner, sticking together as usual, and Maggie could think of nothing worse for she loved mixing with local Italians and finding out about life in Umbria. Some of these ex-pats wanted to live in Italy as if they were in another part of England. They also appeared to be quite heavy drinkers, probably due to boredom.

The flower stall had long-stemmed roses and lilies, which Maggie bought. Then she turned to the vegetable stall and her shopping trolley was soon full. Looking at her watch, she realised she had better return to the cottage in case Daniella was waiting for her. Thrusting the trolley into the boot of the Fiat, she was just shutting the door when a couple said hello to her. She had not seen them before but they were obviously English.

'Hi, are you the Australian?' the woman asked.

'Yes. I am, from Sydney.'

'I'm Rebecca and this is Rupert. I'm Australian too. Where are you from in Sydney?'

'Balmain, but I also lived in Paddington and grew up on the North Shore.'

Maggie chatted to them briefly but she didn't want to be late home. 'Where do you live?'

Rupert handed her a card with their details on it. 'Here's our email and mobile phone number. We live up near Castel Rigone,' he told her.

Maggie was amazed. How lovely to have some Aussies to chat to, and they were about her age.

'Well I'm sorry I have to rush off now as I have a man coming to fix the dishwasher. I will be in touch and we must get together,' she promised.

The couple waved and she put the car into gear and sped off back up the hill.

It might be a good idea to invite them to my party, Maggie thought as she drove. The list of people grew longer each day. However, she still felt nervous about Antonio's parents coming the following day. Once that was out of the way she would feel happier. She knew she would probably come across the ex-girlfriend sometime. It was difficult to live up to someone as beautiful and elegant as that, and the fact she was the daughter of close friends made it more impossible.

Maggie was putting the flowers in water when the crunch of gravel announced the repairman's arrival. Like most of the locals he spoke very little English, and she showed him the dishwasher. Lots of sign language seemed to help. Then she heard Daniella arriving, the dogs barking furiously in the distance. She was glad they weren't allowed to roam. Even so, she often took a walking stick when she walked through the village. Francesca did the same but she was scared stiff of snakes and like to be 'armed.'

Daniella hesitated on the doorstep. Like all the Italians Maggie had met, they were very polite and always asked before they entered.

'*Permesso?*' she asked. *If only people at home were that polite!*

'Ciao, Daniella,' she smiled at the young woman on the doorstep. She led her into the villa as that needed a good clean. The cottage she could easily do herself. She showed Daniella the laundry room and the cleaning utensils. Francesca had advised her that they used big galvanised buckets with a draining hole for the funny string mops they preferred. Maggie opened all the shutters and watched as big, fat black scorpion emerge from one. Daniella quickly dispatched it with a broom handle – it lay squashed on the floor.

They wandered through each room and upstairs to the next floor, the *piano superiore* as she had learnt to call it. Downstairs was the *piano inferiore*. Daniella was full of admiration for what had been achieved as obviously the locals had seen the interior of the house over the years and were intrigued when Maggie's aunt had bought it.

The furniture polish she had bought was the most wonderful scented beeswax, organic and so different from the rubbishy stuff on sale in supermarkets. Maggie had bought from a market stall lots of old rags to use as dusters. The odd thing was there were no second-hand shops around. She and her friends often loved to get a bargain in the op shops in Sydney. Italians obviously didn't 'do' second-hand!

Daniella admired the bathroom with the pretty *Deruta* plates on the wall. They stood out beautifully against the white paintwork. The linen cupboard was full of crisp, clean cotton sheets, and sprigs of lavender were dotted around. Maggie had made up the beds and put pictures on the walls while the cottage was being renovated. She enjoyed picking up pictures and had found an excellent local artist who painted water colours of local scenes. She had found some very attractive mirrors in a hardware shop as well. The table lamps were from Gran Casa and a local man had made the glass-topped iron bedside tables. He was called a *'fabro'* and she was thrilled with his workmanship. He also made her coffee tables that were about twice as heavy as the one she had from IKEA in Sydney!

Daniella was quite happy getting to work and started singing as she did so. She told Maggie she would lock up when she had finished and return the key to her. They agreed to leave the shutters open so the house would be full of light for her visitors.

When Daniella brought the key back Maggie paid her. The girl seemed keen to do whatever work Maggie had in mind and she asked her if she was willing to help with the House Warming Party the following week.

'That is no problem,' she assured Maggie and walked briskly away to her house at the other end of the village, setting the dogs off again as she strode past.

Finally settling down on the sofa to finish her Donna Leon book, Maggie heard the sound of cars driving along the road. She put the book down and checked herself in the mirror. *It's ridiculous! I feel like a teenager on my first date,* she thought.

Antonio appeared at the door, smiling, encouraging her, his parents followed closely behind. Eleanor had brought her a beautiful indoor plant as a house-warming gift. They both murmured *'permesso?'* as they stepped over the threshold.

Antonio gestured Maggie to start the tour of the cottage and she told him she would do so as long as he answered any technical questions his father might ask! They wandered around and Antonio explained the salt filter system in the garage, which made all the water in both buildings soft, and pointed out the alarm system. They were obviously impressed with her small home and Eleanor loved the silk flowers she had bought over the Internet, and the colour of the furnishings.

They then walked over to the villa and spent an hour inspecting that. Paulo was intrigued that the swimming pool was salt-water, which he had never seen before. They both thought the huge sitting room upstairs was grand and were impressed with the building work including the re-pointed stonework. Eleanor asked Maggie if she had any formal training in garden design as they both thought it was beautiful.

'No. I just love gardening and I wanted to make my mark on it. I disliked the idea of someone else designing it.'

'Sadly, I never met your aunt. She bought the villa and had started the work on it when she suddenly died … before I had a chance to contact her.'

'She was a wonderful woman. Very feisty,' said Maggie 'I just hope she approves of what I have done. I was in Australia when she died so all I had were her letters telling me what she was doing.'

They returned to the cottage and Maggie offered them a drink and put the pastries on the coffee table. The men decided on a cold beer; both Eleanor and Maggie chose tea. They settled comfortably on adjoining sofas and Maggie busied herself in the kitchen. Antonio came in to help her and gave her a quick hug. She missed him as he had been very busy and of course had stayed at his parent's house. She hoped he might come and stay up at the cottage but wondered how his parents would take to that idea. She was obviously still under their scrutiny.

Carrying glasses of beer and teacups on a tray, Maggie sensed Eleanor was watching them carefully. Paulo, however, was busy leafing through the technical stuff Antonio had shown him relating to the work on the two buildings. The plunge pool outside the cottage also intrigued him. Obviously Eleanor could see how close Antonio and she had become but his father was engrossed in the data. Maggie told them about the couple she had met briefly in the market and wondered if they knew them.

'Yes, I know them well. They have an Etruscan tomb in their garden,' Eleanor remarked.

'Good heavens! How big is it?' Maggie wanted to know.

'Well I seem to remember it's not huge but you should get to know them and go and see it for yourself. Not many people have Etruscan tombs to show off!'

As they sat enjoying the delicious pastries, Antonio asked her what she had planned for the following week or two. She told him about the visit to *La Foce* which was coming up and Eleanor told her she would absolutely love the garden there.

'There is a wonderful organic café there too, so you must visit that for lunch or coffee. You can also buy Iris Origo's biography and her diary, plus a stunning coffee-table book on *La Foce*. The best time to visit is now when the roses are out but other seasons are good too. Who are you going with?'

'I belong to a Garden Group and we are all going there with a guide. I went on a visit to Fiesole with them not so very long ago.'

'Well, you are settling in well. How is your Italian coming along? I found it very hard years ago when I married Paulo. I had to pick it up myself and I eventually found a class to go to where I learnt the correct grammar.'

'I'm having private lessons but I would like to go to the university in Perugia to do a more advanced course.'

Eleanor looked delighted at this.

'Aren't you going back to live in Australia at all?'

Maggie didn't dare look at Antonio when she answered. 'I have no desire to do so but of course it depends how I cope with the winter here. We don't have very cold winters in Sydney, only in places inland like Canberra. But I know I will love the summer here.'

Paulo looked up from the paperwork, having overheard this. He made no comment but looked at Antonio and then back at Maggie. Maggie hoped he realised they had a strong relationship by the way Antonio looked at her, the way he couldn't resist touching her when he passed; it didn't go unnoticed. Antonio's father didn't look very happy about it but kissed her goodbye when they left.

Maggie breathed with relief. The visit was over.

Antonio held her hand as they walked back into the cottage, and he kissed the top of her head as they closed the door behind them. He drew her over to the sofa and looked into her eyes. With passionate kisses, it wasn't long before they found themselves in her bedroom, all thoughts of dinner vanishing for hours.

They had a meal of leftovers then Antonio said he had better get home as he had an early start in the morning.

'I think I would feel happier staying here with you. I don't really like the idea of you being on your own in the cottage, even with people staying in the villa,' he said, stroking her hair.

Maggie touched his cheek. 'And I would like nothing better than you being with me too.'

He reluctantly left telling her he would come back tomorrow evening and stay. He would tell his parents tonight and, if they objected, that was their problem. Maggie felt so much happier and more at ease. *Thank goodness he can stand up to them if they don't like the idea and don't want us to be together. It's such a shame this has affected his business relationship with his partner.'*

The next morning she had a reply from Geoffrey. Her lovely old Historian friend was delighted to be invited to the party and wondered if she minded him bringing someone who would drive him home. That was good news. She then had replies from the Garden Group. Everyone was able to come. Of course, at this time of the year many of the members had left for warmer climes, which meant there were fewer people around to invite. Francesca and Gino were coming, and so were the couple who owned the Etruscan tomb. She looked forward to talking with Rebecca about Australia.

Francesca rang with news that the vet had been to visit the kennels and had issued a warning to the owners, and the *carabiniere* had been seen visiting the house. Something was definitely happening there, Francesco had heard from the neighbours. She said she and Gino would try and discover more when they went for a walk later on in the evening. No one liked the people who lived there but all were wary of them.

Antonio rang just as she finished her tea. He asked if she would meet him for a meal in the wine bar then he would come up afterwards and stay the night. She felt happy hearing from him, as she wanted to hear his parents' opinion of the restoration work. She knew Antonio appreciated his father's advice and she tried not to worry about what they thought of her. She put that out of her mind till later on when she could discuss things with Antonio in person. Busying herself, she put out fresh towels in the bathroom and tidied up, then pondered what to wear.

Driving down the hill, Maggie noticed the man with the black horse standing watching the road. It felt a bit unsettling; he was strange. And she hadn't seen him riding the horse lately. She asked Francesca about him and was told he had an unrequited love affair with someone in the village and was a very unhappy man.

When she reached the wine bar, she went in and asked the owner to keep a table free for the two of them, and sat chatting with them amicably while enjoying a glass of wine. When Antonio arrived, he kissed her on both cheeks, and greeted the bar owners who he knew well. He ordered a glass of red and they checked the blackboard menu. Veal escalope was on offer, a big favourite. It was the end of the season for tomatoes and they enjoyed cooked tomatoes drizzled with olive oil and balsamic vinegar, with *scaloppino* potatoes scattered with rosemary.

'Well what did your parents think of the restoration work?'

'They loved it. And they liked your decorating skills. Interestingly, my mother also seemed happier about our relationship, as she realises you are not just a summer visitor.'

That sounds promising. She'd been so worried they would still be critical of her and could understand that a 'blow in' wouldn't be the number one choice for Antonio.

'But your father is not so happy about us, is he?'

'No but then they were in a similar situation when they parents met, which they conveniently forget. They met on holiday on a beach on the *Amalfi* coast and my father was actually engaged to someone else at the time! It caused a big row with his own parents because they thought he had dishonoured the family.'

Maggie's jaw dropped. *They really have no right to judge Antonio and his relationship then!* She took another sip of her wine and gazed across the table at him. He looked a bit shell-shocked after their confrontation.

'Well how long are you going to stay at the cottage with me?' she asked him.

'As long as you'll have me or throw me out!' he laughed. When the owner asked them if they would like anything else, they shook their heads. They really wanted to get back to the cottage and be on their own. Antonio asked for the bill.

'*Il conto, per favore.*' The bar owner took the card from Antonio, and smiled indulgently at them. He could see they were in love, and all Italians adore a love story.

They drove back up the hill in convoy. Maggie had opened her window to let the fresh air in, to let it blow her happiness all across Umbria. She'd been so fixated on his parents' attitude, and now it seemed to have been resolved. How weird that his father in particular had been so difficult when the same thing had happened with his wife. It had been much worse too as he was actually engaged to someone else! *What short memories some people have.*

They parked their cars, and Maggie led the way in, turning off the alarm as she went. They closed the door and fell into each other's arms. Antonio picked her up and carried her to the bedroom, where they undressed each other and collapsed onto the bed. Antonio nibbled her ears and she was lost in a haze of desire. She couldn't wait for him to make love to her properly. They clung to each other and she almost exploded with love for this man. His every move was like an electrical current going through her. After, they kissed and fell asleep lying in each other's arms.

Next morning Antonio rose first and made coffee, putting hers beside the bed.

'I would love to join you back in bed, but someone has to go and earn their salary!' he grinned before disappearing into the bathroom.

Just before he left, Maggie asked, 'Do you think your parents would enjoy coming to the party?'

He smiled warmly. 'I can't see why not. Call them.'

Eleanor answered the phone and she sounded delighted to be asked. They were free and would attend. 'I love what you have done with the villa and the cottage. Your ideas and mine are so alike. Not too over the top, which some Italian homes can be.'

Maggie thanked her for her comments. She liked Eleanor enormously and was glad they seemed to get on.

Maggie spent the day shopping for the party, which was the next evening and then time just flew.

The party was a great success and Daniella had been a great help. Antonio had enjoyed talking to Geoffrey and they had chatted for ages about the area's history. Eleanor and Paulo had met Francesca and her family, and the Garden Group had also mixed well, and reminded Maggie about the visit to *La Foce* the following week.

Once the leftover food had all been put in the fridge Antonio and she walked back to the cottage, tired but happy. Any other clearing up could be left till the morning

.

&

Chapter Fourteen

Helen and George picked Maggie up for the visit to La Foce. They set off early, as it was a good hour and a half's drive away. The meeting place was the restaurant run by one of the Origo family which was well known serving organic food. Once gathered, the group sat outside enjoying the sunshine, and the company, and raving about the delicious food. After lunch they drove in convoy to the villa nearby.

After parking the car, Helen and George guided Maggie towards the entrance of a stunning cream-coloured villa where they were given their tickets, A guide welcomed them and asked if they wished her to speak in Italian or English. As everyone spoke English that was the choice. She showed them around the huge courtyard and wonderfully laid out gardens and explained that the famous English designer, Pinsent, designed them. They walked through various 'rooms' in the gardens and stood looking over to the famous zig-zag road in the distance. The structure of the garden could easily be seen, especially the gorgeous wisteria arbour, and the roses were magnificent. Finally she took them to the private cemetery where family members were interred in a very peaceful setting.

'It's hard to imagine the terrifying ordeal Iris Origo went through with the *contradini* (peasants) when the Germans invaded. They risked their lives saving allied airmen who'd been shot down, didn't they?' Maggie asked Helen.

Helen nodded. 'It makes riveting reading in her diary. She ran a small school and hospital here for children affected by the war as well as helping those airmen. With Italy being in on both sides of the war, it was easy to see whose side they were on.'

At the end of the tour, Maggie purchased the beautiful coffee table book of La Foce, Iris Origo's Diary and her biography, and vowed she would come back in both the winter and spring to show the gardens to Antonio.

Maggie invited Helen and George in for supper on their return and Antonio soon joined them. He rang the doorbell just as they settled down with a glass of wine. The couple had met Antonio briefly at the party but it was interesting to see how they interacted now, George and Helen being terribly English despite living in Italy for so many years. Antonio could put on his 'English demeanour' when he wanted but sometimes he was very Italian which was an interesting mix. He declined a drink until it was time to eat, as his job would suffer greatly if he lost his licence.

Maggie served smoked salmon on blinis and went to the stove to check on the pasta. She was giving them *orecchiette* – ear-shaped pasta with thin strips of pork in a creamy sauce with coriander – this followed by a cheeseboard with a huge variety of cheeses. The cheese man in the market was excellent and she loved the stronger pecorino cheese she bought there, as well as the delicious dolce latte Gorgonzola.

They sat at the dining room table, which was the bane of Maggie's life. She knew that a glass-topped dining table would be difficult, but it looked perfect in its setting even if it showed every mark.

Talk turned to La Foce and the war and what a hard time many Italians had endured. Antonio knew a lot about it having uncles and grandparents living through the horrors and the hardships.

'Anyway it's all in the past and the Germans come here now and enjoy Italy. The European Union has helped everyone get on so well together and having an EU passport is so useful.'

He told Helen and George about his experiences working in England and the evening went quickly. George looked at his watch after they had finished the cheese course and said they should be on their way. He was getting older and disliked driving in the dark. They waved them off and walked back into the cottage, arm in arm.

Chapter Fifteen

Maggie's friends emailed to say their plans had changed and they couldn't visit after all which she was quite glad about as she had so much to do to get the villa ready for summer visitors. Perhaps if she were here next year, she could organise for friends to visit. It would be lovely to have them when she had more time on her hands.

Right now she had bookings for the villa mainly from the UK and Germany, the first tenants arriving at the weekend. It couldn't be too soon as, even with the money from rentals, her bank balance was so low and it would be hard to break even.

'I know there is something bothering you. Are you going to tell me or not?' he asked one evening.

Maggie was reluctant to share her woes, but Antonio squeezed her hand reassuringly. 'Well I am worried,' she finally said. 'My darling aunt left everything to me, including money for the restoration but it has taken so much longer to get it finished the bank balance has really run down. It's odd because everyone thought she was much wealthier than she obviously was.'

'Have you checked with the bank in London to see if she had other accounts?' Antonio suggested.

'Well I suppose she could have had more money hidden away but I would have thought her lawyer would know that.'

'I suggest you try and find out. Is it that serious that you can't carry on?'

'I'm afraid so. I have worked out that the rentals will bring in just so much, but it is not enough, and I dread having to sell it. It is increasingly looking more like it though. House prices are still quite low too.'

'Well we can always live in my parents' house if the worst happens,' Antonio said, ruffling her hair.

'I don't think so. They are still very unsure about me, and I know it has caused a huge rift with your father and his friend. I wouldn't feel happy doing that.'

'You know my mother likes you, but I do agree, my father was deeply disappointed in the breakup with Livia. It's not personal but he had it firmly in his mind that I was going to marry her and join the two families together.'

It was a worrying dilemma on both sides.

The next day, Antonio worked in Perugia until late so Maggie rang the lawyer who had drawn up her aunt's Will. When she finally reached him in London, he exclaimed that he'd been trying to contact her. There were more papers to sign and matters to be finalised.

'Did you write to my address in Australia?' Maggie enquired. 'Why didn't you send them there?'

'I did. I sent them by airmail too, but never had a reply,' the lawyer said.

'How odd. I thought my flat mates would have sent them on to me. Anyway, do you need me to fly to London or can I sort out things from here?'

'Well, as long as you get your signature verified by a lawyer in Italy, that would be fine. There is no need to come to London.'

''Just what do these papers entail?' she frowned.

147

'Your aunt had an account in the Channel Islands and it took quite a while to sort out all the formalities since she died in Italy and not in Britain. We need to transfer the funds from her account there to you. Where would you like it to be sent? Also, these days we have many formalities to consider regarding money-laundering laws. I also didn't have your email address.'

At the mention of another account, Maggie's heart leapt. She wondered how much it would be. She didn't want to get her hopes up too high but managed to stop her hands shaking. Perhaps her prayers and candles in Assisi had worked!

'I have my own bank account here in Italy. What sort of sum are we talking about? I'm very surprised as I didn't know anything about this.'

'Well I am glad we are in touch now and please give me your email address so I can write to you. It is somewhere in the region of £300,000.'

Maggie almost fell on the floor. Not in her wildest dreams had she thought she would have the answer to her prayers – it was more than she could possibly have imagined. How wonderful if she didn't have to sell the villa.

That night, when Antonio returned to the cottage, she greeted him with a wide smile. A bottle of Prosecco was on ice and he raised his eyebrows.

'Good news?'

'Fantastic news! There was a bank account I didn't know about in the Channel Islands and once the money is transferred to me here the villa will be safe!' She flung her arms around his neck.

'Ti amo! Sono così felice per te!'

'Yes, I didn't want to let my darling aunt down and I feel so much better that I can concentrate on running it as a proper business. It is such a relief to be able to stop worrying.' Then she burst into tears.

Antonio gathered her into his arms. 'Whatever makes you happy is fine with me,' he mused. He kissed her and together they discussed the future.

The bookings for the villa were looking healthy. The first family had arrived at the weekend, flying into Perugia. They had hired a car and were enthusiastically touring the area. They told Maggie they just loved the scenery and the village. The pool was a great attraction too and their young children spent many happy hours in it. They told her they had holidayed in Tuscany before but now preferred Umbria.

'I can see why it is called the Green Heart of Italy,' the father told her. 'It is so beautiful and green and not as hot as where we stayed before near Siena where there are fewer trees around.'

Maggie still wondered why she hadn't received the mail from the lawyer, so she rang her flat mates in Sydney. It was time to tell them she wasn't coming back.

'Hi Ruth, it's Maggie,' she said when the call connected.

'Well stone the crows … is it raining there like it is here?'

No, it's summer here and I'm glad I'm not enduring your wet weather,' Maggie laughed. 'I have a couple of things to tell you but first of all did you receive some mail for me from London?'

'Yes, we did and stupidly Jenny, who is sub-letting your room, put your name and Italian address on it, and re-directed it. She didn't put more stamps on it so it would have gone by sea mail. I hope it wasn't important.'

'Well, yes actually, it was. I still haven't received it but it was from my aunt's lawyer in London. Why on earth didn't she put it in an airmail bag and I could easily have sent her the money to reimburse her?'

'No idea. She is an artist so her head is in the clouds I reckon. Very sorry about it though, as you know Jan or I would have done the right thing, even if they had charged like wounded bulls for it!'

Maggie couldn't be cross. Listening to her flat mate's lovely Aussie accent actually made her homesick.

'Well it's sorted now as I rang him in the UK and he and I are now conversing via email.'

'Well, what is your other news then?'

'I'm staying on here as I love Italy, but more importantly, I have fallen in love with an Italian guy,' Maggie told her.

'Wow! That is a turn up for the books. Good grief! Wait till I tell the others. No one else is here now as it's still early so we might have to go to the pub to celebrate.'

'Yes, sorry I meant to tell you earlier. It's all very romantic and of course I said I would never fall for an Italian but his mother is English so perhaps that makes a difference.'

'Gee, I am so pleased for you and Jan will be too. Do you want Jenny to keep on renting your room then and we can put her on the lease properly?'

'Yes I think that's wise. I will tell you all more about everything in an email.' By that she meant the difficulty with his parents.

After she put the phone down, she felt sad that she hadn't seen the girls for such a long time. She really enjoyed their company.

Antonio over the past few months had tried to reason with his father about their relationship but it was hard going. His mother seemed happy for them, and it wasn't until Livia landed a modelling job in New York that things improved. She was so intent on her career that nothing else mattered, and her father was thrilled he could boast about his beautiful New York-based model daughter. Marrying an Italian geometra was now something he wasn't too worried about. The dynamics had changed.

Antonio breathed a sigh of relief.

The weather had now become autumnal. As many people told Maggie, it was the best time of the year in Italy.

'Have you ever been to a *vendemmia?*' Antonio asked her.

She shook her head. 'No. What on earth is that?'

'It's the grape harvest. It is not really that much hard work but it is good fun. If you would like to, you can help friends by lending a hand at the harvest and they give you lunch too. It's a very sociable event.'

'I would love to do that. I enjoyed fruit picking when I was a child. We enjoyed going to my grandmother's in Victoria, picking strawberries and other fruits but we ate almost as many as we gathered!'

'Well I have a friend with a vineyard and we could go along one Saturday and help. He is a keen musician and they will have people entertaining us at lunchtime as well. The wine is not the best but you can always water it down!'

Maggie enjoyed the physical work in the fresh air, and had always enjoyed fruit picking. They were all given baskets, and rows of people chatted, laughed and sang while picking the grapes. Antonio was near Maggie in the same row, but not as quick as she was at stripping the vines. She enjoyed it enormously and couldn't believe when a bell sounded that it was lunchtime. They all emptied their baskets into a big trailer and the women walked into the house to freshen up. The men all disappeared in the direction of the barns, as there was an outside ablutions there where they splashed their faces to cool down. Maggie stood in line to freshen up and managed a brief conversation in mixed languages with an Italian girl. Lavinia was her name and she was interested to meet Antonio's new girlfriend and was amazed Maggie had come all the way from Australia.

'I remember meeting Antonio's old girlfriend years ago,' she said.

'Oh yes, she is now a model in New York,' Maggie told her.

'Oh well, that will suit her. She was always looking in the mirror!' The girl laughed and Maggie smiled, knowing what she meant.

Lunch was served on rough outdoor tables: bowls of pasta, spinach tarts, and bottles of homemade wine for the taking. As Antonio had warned her, the wine was a bit rough so she diluted it with bottled water. Italians all seemed to drink bottled water. During lunch, a group of young opera singers entertained them, making it a truly magical day. Maggie felt she'd been transported back in time, and guessed this was how vendemmias had been conducted for hundreds of years. Italians certainly knew how to enjoy life. The sky was blue and although the morning had a sharp nip in the air, it had grown quite hot by the time they sat down at the table. The hills were bathed in warm sunshine and the leaves on the trees were beginning to turn a beautiful golden brown.

At the end of the meal, Antonio and Maggie chatted to the owners who were grateful of their help. Then they drove off down the driveway, both tired after a busy day in the fresh air.

Maggie ruefully looked at her hands, which were stained with grape juice. She would have to soak them to clean them up when she got home. As they reached a layby on the road, Antonio pulled over to show her the view. As she turned back to him, he reached over and kissed her.

September was a beautiful month in Italy, one that meant clear days with blue skies and fewer tourists around. After the grapes had been harvested, the next big event was picking olives. This was usually done in November when the weather wasn't so pleasant and was often cool and raining. It was too cold to swim in the pool but was a good month to visit cities like Rome and Florence, and the weather was ideal for walking. People still wanted to book the villa in September and even into October. After that, the bookings ceased.

Olive picking was the next big local event. Francesca's parents and a few others were happy to help pick her olives and give her a container of olive oil. All the villagers sent the olives to the local *frantoio*, the building she could just see from the villa. It was a lovely old stone building where they crushed the olives and made oil, the establishment run by the son of one of the old ladies in the village. This would be starting in a few days' time. She had seen the pickers gathering olives the old-fashioned way in a nearby village, using nets. Big olive farms of course used mechanical methods to get the olive harvest in, but the best olive oil was made using the old way she'd been told. According to the owner of the local wine bar, the finest olive oil came from around Spoleto; another place for Maggie to explore and she had heard about the beautiful basilica there.

After tidying the garden and checking around the buildings to make sure all was neat and tidy before winter came, Maggie made a pot of tea, poured it into a bone china teacup, which must have been a hangover from her late mother's English family. Putting her feet up, she relaxed on the sofa, flicking through a copy of the '*Australian Women's Weekly*' magazine. The local postmistress who came in her little Fiat van had delivered this copy today. She often waved to her as she passed her on the twisting road down to town. Maggie smiled, remembering the postie in Sydney who rode a motor bike and wore a Legionnaire type hat to keep the sun off! How different life was here.

Antonio came home to find her engrossed in her magazine.

'Are you feeling homesick for Australia?' he asked.

'Well definitely with this weather at the moment,' she laughed. 'No, not really but I would love to go back sometime.'

The rentals over the summer had been consistent and Maggie was already organising the website for the following summer. She hoped to get someone in for a winter tenancy, as she understood it was sensible to keep the old houses warm and dry if possible. An advertisement had gone into a magazine in Britain and she was hoping for a reply. Renting it out wasn't as important as keeping the house aired. Perhaps someone like a writer might like the peace and quiet.

Soon the olive picking had finished, everyone having joined in. Maggie hadn't enjoy it very much as it had been quite chilly and drizzled often. However, she really looked forward to having her own olive oil. The vendemmia was much more fun as the weather then was warmer.

Antonio's parents invited them for Sunday lunch and, although she loved seeing his mother, she was still wary of his father. It was taking a long time to be accepted by him.

The day turned out to be cold but with a glorious blue sky and bright sunshine. She dressed in a light wool dress and wore her new long elegant, black leather boots. Antonio was always complimenting her and noticing what she wore – very different compared to self-absorbed Jonathan. Maggie had only heard from him once since she'd seen him in the spring, and he had found a wealthy girlfriend, which didn't surprise her in the least.

When they arrived, both Antonio's parents greeted them on the doorstep and hugged her. Their beautiful retriever dog enthusiastically wagged its tail, nearly knocking her over. The atmosphere was so much warmer than before and Maggie felt more at home. Antonio's father definitely made more of an effort and she sensed Antonio was more relaxed too given the change in him. When she went into the kitchen to help his mother bring out the meal, she overheard his father talking about his business partner and friend. The fact that Livia was such a success in New York had mended bridges.

Antonio and his mother had an intimate conversation after lunch while his father was very interested to hear how the season's bookings had gone for Maggie. Thankfully, feeling lunch had been a success, they drove contentedly home to the cottage. The skies had become darker and it was definitely feeling wintry. The cottage was cosy though and much easier to heat than the villa.

Early next morning snow fell and made the ground looked pretty. Maggie loved to see snow and rushed out with her iPad so she could send photos back to the flat-mates in Sydney. Antonio suggested they have a meal out in a well-known restaurant not far from Perugia then drove off to work. The restaurant had gained quite a few stars and was situated in an old castle. He said he would book one evening soon and kissed her on the cheek as he rushed off.

Maggie had never driven in snow and therefore drove gingerly down the hill to buy in supplies. She thought it wise to stock up in case there was more snow to come. Before she left, Antonio rang on her mobile. He'd managed to get a cancellation for the next night at the restaurant. Maggie was thrilled but then wondered what she would wear.

The weather was quite cold now and she decided to check out one of the smarter shops in town while she was down there. She browsed around, then found the ideal dress, a dark aubergine, ankle length, long sleeved dress in velvet. With its low-cut, square neckline, it looked very smart, and the price was right. She decided to drive to the Mall just outside Perugia to have a look for shoes to match. There was an excellent shoe shop there with a large supermarket nearby so could get all the shopping she needed in one place.

As the sky turned dark she hastened back home, driving as carefully as she could. Going up the hill to the cottage the road was very slippery and she was relieved to arrive safely. She dashed inside to the warmth and was thankful she had left the central heating on. She lit the wood stove, which meant that the central heating didn't need to be on too long, and made herself a cup of tea. She loved the wood stove – it was a really good investment – and just looking at the flames made her feel warm. She smiled to think she had found Sydney cold in the winter!

Antonio came home early as he was worried about the snow, but the forecast said it would ease in the morning, with no more snow forecast for the next few days. That was a relief seeing they were going out the following evening for dinner. Antonio suggested it might be wise to stay the night and rang and booked a room.

The next morning the sun glistened on the snow making it look even more pretty but it also made it melt quite quickly. In the late afternoon, Maggie luxuriated in the bath then dressed in her new finery. Antonio, who had left work early, arrived home, showered and changed into his *Ermenegildo Zegna* suit. He looked incredibly handsome.

'Wow!' he said when Maggie modelled her new outfit for him. 'I wonder if we should just stay home. You look so wonderful I won't be able to keep my hands off you.' He smiled.

Maggie laughed and, taking his hand in hers, squeezed it. 'I think we had better get going or else I'll have to slap you down!'

They picked up their overnight bags and hurried out to the car, which still had a smattering of snow across the roof and bonnet. The air was crisp and cold and they were glad of the heater when they set off. It was only about a forty minute drive but it could become tricky if the weather turned nasty.

They drove through the castle gates and parked under a canopy by the front door. A bellboy rushed out and advised he would park the car for them, and carried their bags into the foyer. Antonio checked in at Reception while Maggie stood admiring the wonderful old building. A huge stone staircase wound up from the foyer and a massive chandelier hung from the ceiling. Soft music played in the background. Through a wide doorway a few people already sat at the bar.

They were shown up to their room where Maggie freshened up, applying more lipstick and splashing her favourite *Guerlain* perfume on her wrists. When staying in hotels she had to carry her passport, while Antonio flashed his carta d'identita. Maggie would be able to get one of those once she applied to the commune.

Musing how her life had changed in the last year, she now felt that Australia was a different world, and smiled at how easily she had slipped into her new life. Her aunt would be delighted.

They wandered downstairs to enjoy an aperitif before dinner and, because they were staying the night, Antonio was more relaxed about drinking. Nevertheless, Maggie sensed he had something on his mind. Maggie caught him frowning slightly and a slight chill crept over her that he wasn't entirely happy in their relationship. Something wasn't quite right. After a Campari and orange she too relaxed and put her worries aside. They were ushered to their table and nodded at the other occupants of the room. Again everyone murmured 'Buono sera' to them. What a long time ago it seemed since she first stayed at the hotel in Tuoro and was introduced to Italian courtesy.

Smiling, Maggie read the menu in Italian, and understood nearly all of it. Practising her Italian on Antonio and being corrected on her pronunciation had made her much more confident in the language. Looking up, she caught Antonio looking at her in amazement. She smiled and when he smiled back, her heart felt as if it had dropped into her shoes. She knew she was in love with this man.

They chatted about the prospect of a winter tenant in the villa, and how useful it would be having someone living there and paying rent. Meanwhile, waiters, almost unnoticed, refilled their wine glasses without fuss. They had chosen a beautiful Barolo wine from Piedmont in Northern Italy. The meal of consommé, and medallions of pork was superb – they both declined the pasta – and finished with a rather sweet zabaglione.

Antonio ordered Maggie a *Limoncello* while he had a glass of cognac. He looked down at the napkin on his lap and Maggie started worrying again about what he was going to say. He had gone serious again. Thoughts of not seeing him and returning to Australia suddenly flashed through her mind. Although his mother had accepted her, she still felt slightly uneasy with his father, and wondered if his father had issued him an ultimatum. She thought that was all over with, but Italians were so family-minded. Many Italians married and came to live in the family home. That, she felt, was a bridge too far.

'Maggie.' Antonio paused and she heard him draw a deep breath. 'I want to ask you something.'

She looked up, not wanting to see the seriousness on his face.

'Yes. What is it?'

"Are you happy living in Umbria? Do you miss Australia?'

She smiled warmly. 'Oh Antonio, I love it here. I do miss Australia sometimes and maybe I will go back sometime, but only for a holiday.'

He breathed in deeply again, and let it out. 'I am pleased as I don't want you to go back there to live. I want you to marry me, Maggie, and stay here. Would you do me the honour of becoming my wife?'

Maggie's jaw dropped. Had she heard correctly? She had worried he wanted to cool their relationship, especially with his father's attitude. A smile spread over her face and Antonio breathed a sigh of utter relief.

Taking a small box out of his pocket, he prised out the ring and slid it on her finger.

'Is that the right finger? I hope you like it. It belonged to my maternal grandmother and is very old.'

The ring had a stunning emerald set in an antique gold band. 'Oh Antonio, it is absolutely gorgeous.' She looked into his eyes. 'Of course I would love to marry you … but what about your parents? I didn't think they wanted this … your father …'

Antonio smiled. 'My mother is very happy that I was going to ask you and that is why she gave me the ring for you. My father is pleased too, as his partner is now only interested in the celebrity model his daughter is becoming. They are friends again and I am sure he will learn to love you too.'

As he put his arm around her, Maggie snuggled in to him. There was nothing more she wanted in this world and wished her aunt could see her absolute happiness.

Other books by this author:

What a Life!

About the Author

Marianne was born in Northern Ireland but grew up in London. She was very interested in travel and enjoyed her time in Bermuda and later in both New Zealand and Australia. Sailing was her passion and living near the water has always been a priority.

Being denied a place at Art School by her parents, she completed a secretarial course which she hated. However, it stood her in good stead when she became a medical secretary and could work anywhere in the world. Marianne married her Naval Officer boyfriend and had two daughters. They all now live in Western Australia. She has twice coped with breast cancer and has five grandchildren whom she adores.

*****

Printed in Australia
AUHW010129250520
328239AU00016B/71

9 781876 922825